STORIES

Celebrating
30 Years of Publishing
in India

STORIES WE NEVER TELL

SAVI SHARMA

HarperCollins *Publishers* India

First published in 2019

This edition published in India by
HarperCollins *Publishers* in 2022
4th Floor, Tower A, Building No 10, DLF Cyber City,
DLF Phase II, Gurugram, Haryana – 122002
www.harpercollins.co.in

2 4 6 8 10 9 7 5 3 1

P-ISBN: 978-93-5629-329-8
E-ISBN: 978-93-5629-330-4

Typeset in Sabon Roman by SŪRYA, New Delhi

Printed and bound at
Thomson Press (India) Ltd

DEDICATED TO

Everyone who still searches for hope and happiness in the forgotten world of books

There are stories of loss, darkness and destruction.
But then there are always stories of hope, light and recovery,
waiting to be told.

PROLOGUE

A simpler time; a time when life didn't move at this frenetic pace, when love meant something, and what you owned was worth less than who you came home to. When people measured their wealth by the number of people in their lives that truly loved them and who they loved in return.

When life wasn't about what someone wore or where they lived. When family and friends mattered, and a person's pain meant something other than someone else's entertainment. Technology and social media were supposed to bring us closer together, to help us identify and understand that we are not alone, but somehow it has become twisted, skewed into a show of how many materialistic items one person can accumulate and how much abuse another can take. We watch and wait for them to slip, to fall, as confirmation of their humanity. To make us feel better about our own imperfections as human beings.

And in the end? When all is said and done, will it matter? What possessions you owned, what car you drove, how many people pretended to care. Does any of this madness mean anything other than that we once breathed? I don't think it does. I think all that matters is that we were happy and that we were loved. That there were people, not things, surrounding us when times were dark, and that somehow, we always managed to find our way back when we were lost.

I

JHANVI

Heartbreak. Have you ever felt it? The undeniable pain; a moment, a realisation, changes the course of your life. When one action, whether it is your own or that of another, forces you to choose. Choosing between leaving them behind or clinging to a memory of what was. Heartbreak. A human condition, a threat to our sanity that only takes a moment to change our lives.

I had found out about Puneet's latest fling through a friend. After he was caught the first time, he promised that it was just a temporary slip: he'd had too much to drink, and the girl had come on to him. In the ensuing confrontation and fall out, Puneet had insinuated that I set him up for failure. I had somehow led him into making out with the girl at the club because of my lifestyle. I had, of course, denied this to begin with, telling my boyfriend that I would not take responsibility for his infidelity, but fighting with him to get my point across was tiring. My life—or certainly the latter part of my teenage years and now as an adult—was spent avoiding conflict. Not that I lacked the backbone to stand up for myself. But my sense of self told me that my words hurt people, and hurting people meant that I was imperfect. A fate worse than death, as far as I was concerned.

Eventually, I relented and promised Puneet I would try and be more considerate to him when we were out in public. This was my third relationship since my social media profile had exploded online. His indiscretion hurt me, forced me to build walls around my heart and, in hindsight, I was guarded, a little bent but not yet broken by him. The fact that he said I made him feel like a failure, that my actions had set him up for those feelings, hit hard. I never wanted to make anyone feel that way because I had spent my life trying to avoid failure in the pursuit of perfection.

My first boyfriend was unable to understand the complexities of being online all the time and eventually broke up with me, saying I was emotionally unavailable because I was so preoccupied with keeping up appearances. He was my high school sweetheart, and when he walked out of my life, it hurt; not just because I lost him as a follower, but because I saw a future with him, complete with two perfect children. He was my whole life, and to him, I was only a chapter in his life. Merely some words to complete his story. I was lonely after Aarav left, and I found myself in the arms of another suitor not long after. Gaurav popped up in my inbox with messages of adoration and promises of a formidable future. He too had a large social media following and understood what I needed to do to push myself into becoming a top influencer. We had fun, taking pictures and posing as the perfect couple for six months, before the cracks began to show in our relationship. Our days were filled taking couples' photos under crisp white sheets with 'good morning!' captions and other meticulously planned pictures in various locations. We barely communicated otherwise, and that suited me. I was never a great talker anyway.

When I finally asked Gaurav about the girls in his various inboxes, he shut me down.

'This is part of the business, Jhanvi. Surely you have just as many male admirers in your inboxes?' Gaurav had laughed it off.

I tried to find my voice, to fight back, but somewhere along the line, I had lost my ability to stand up for myself. Instead of pushing back and demanding a change in his behaviour, I accepted his explanation. I did have plenty of men sending me messages, everything from declarations of love to unsavoury photos of their genitalia. The difference was that I did not entertain them the way Gaurav did. I felt like I was in constant competition with a world of women. It drove me to pursue perfection even more relentlessly, in a bid to show them that they were not in my league.

It wasn't all bad, though. Gaurav's followers began to filter onto my social media slowly, my following grew steadily, and he taught me how to work the system. It wasn't long before we were being let into clubs and restaurants free of charge, as long as we documented it online. In a way, I always knew that he was not one hundred per cent faithful to me, and I accepted that. He provided a good life for me, and he was helping me build my career; as long as it stayed out of the public eye, I was all right with it.

One day, a short video clip began to circulate on social media. It showed Gaurav getting out of a girl's bed naked, and walking towards the camera. The girl, a relatively unknown social media entity, posted it online. Overnight, she became a sensation, while my life fell apart.

'Do you have any idea what you have done?' I screamed at Gaurav. As usual, the wrong words came out. 'You have destroyed me! Destroyed us!' I couldn't stop the wave of emotion that was screaming to be let out. I didn't want a fight, I was ready to admit defeat the moment I saw the post online, but I was humiliated.

'You are always so dramatic, Jhanvi,' he said, his mouth curved into a cocky smile as if he was enjoying my pain. 'You have always known what this life brings with it, and you aren't exactly pure and innocent either,' he continued, ignoring my tears. His smug expression was all I needed to see him for who he really was.

Online, sides were picked, and a few times after the initial outburst, I did try to tell Gaurav how betrayed I felt. But, ultimately, I couldn't find the inner strength to get my point across. Comments flew around online about how the girl was nothing special. Gaurav occupied a different girl's bed every other day. I let out a breath I didn't realise I was holding. Our relationship was over, but I had no idea what kind of damage would be done to our reputation—or my reputation, specifically.

I was humiliated, but I did not feel the emotional devastation I had when Aarav split up with me. The day I decided I could not bear it any longer, the words finally came. 'Sleeping with these other women is so disrespectful to our relationship, Gaurav. We are two people who decided to commit to each other. I trusted you, and you betrayed me.'

He tried to apologise, but it was too late. In the aftermath, I filled my time online posting excuses for why my relationship had deteriorated, and building a facade that everything was all right. Behind the scenes, I plunged myself into my work, watching how my followers increased and how the demographics changed from young women trying to emulate me to young men trying to offer me some comfort.

And then, there was Puneet. I didn't meet him online; I decided after Gaurav to shy away from any man with a popular online profile. We met on a bus, and he didn't know who I was, which I found intriguing. At the beginning of our relationship, I hid my social media presence from him. Eventually, as our relationship progressed, I had to be honest with him. I needed to make social appearances, even if they were few and far between. Slowly, Puneet was introduced to my lifestyle: restaurants, clubs, clothing. I enjoyed dressing him up and introducing him to my followers and my world. But as he became more involved in my life, he also became more distant from me. He was more concerned about what people thought about him than my presence in his life. Days spent wandering

Savi Sharma

the markets, holding hands and having deep conversations were replaced with superficial shots of us pretending to be in love. And it wasn't that I didn't love him, I just wished he would pay the same amount of attention to me as he did when we first began our courtship.

His first indiscretion happened in front of me. Admittedly, his statement that he was drinking heavily was true. We went out for a club opening; all expenses paid, of course. I made it a rule not to drink when I was on the job. Sure, I would pose with a glass of champagne or whatever was offered, but I never actually drank what was given to me. That particular appearance was Puneet's first introduction to a big event where everything was paid for. The alcohol flowed freely in the VIP area, and it wasn't long before the usual crowd of hangers-on made their way over to try and integrate themselves into the 'influencer' crowd. Puneet, who was already slightly intoxicated at that stage, welcomed in a group of girls who quickly made themselves more comfortable than they should have.

I busied myself with photos of the great time I was having. Selfies and group shots with club-goers were put into swipe stories which featured videos of the DJ playing music—all to show how grand the party was. I could not include Puneet in these stories, though; he was too drunk. Instead, I tasked him with staying in the VIP area to socialise with the groupies.

I was dancing on the main stage when I caught sight of what was happening. Being careful not to draw negative attention to myself, I made my way through the crowded main dance area and up the stairs to the VIP section. As I reached the landing, one of the two groupie girls I had seen from the stage swung her leg over Puneet's lap and mounted him, before kissing him deeply. I was in total shock; I couldn't move for a few seconds. My feet were glued to the floor like I was standing in thick mud, unable to move forward or choose to step away.

'He will push her off,' I told myself, but it never happened. Instead, he seemed to pull the girl closer to him. Feelings of humiliation from Gaurav's betrayals flooded through my brain as I launched myself out of my frozen state. By the time I reached my boyfriend and the girl, a friend had pulled her off Puneet's lap. I remained composed.

'It's time for you ladies to go,' I said, my gaze never leaving Puneet. Dignity and grace were essential to avoid any further online gossip about my love life. Even though what I really wanted to do was explode in rage. Puneet stood up to try and defend himself, but he was so drunk that he staggered and swayed before sitting down again.

'You are drunk and embarrassing. Please don't leave the VIP area until I'm back,' I managed to say calmly, before requesting a nearby waitress to bring sweet black coffee and water for him. I also asked that the bouncer not allow any more groupies into the VIP area. I was able to keep my composure as I walked through the crowd and into the ladies' room, even stopping to pose with a group of men who wanted a picture.

'Selfie?' they asked, and then, not waiting for an answer, they draped their sweaty arms heavily across my shoulders.

'Sure,' I muttered, although I knew that my answer was unheard.

'You are quite beautiful,' one man leaned into me and shouted over the music. This time I couldn't respond with anything other than a smile. The weight of their arms on me seemed only to amplify the weight that was pressing against my chest.

The ladies' room was full of chattering girls applying lipstick and posing for photos next to the stylish chaise longue. I found a free stall and escaped inside. Once the stall door closed, a flood of tears erupted. In my mind, I formulated a plan of how

I could deny yet another cheating boyfriend online. Hopefully, no one had taken photos of Puneet's make-out session. But I had to be honest with myself—it was doubtful.

'Get yourself together, Jhanvi,' I whispered, opening my bag. I removed my compact and re-applied my makeup. Dark brown eyes, almost black, looked back at me as I touched up the thick kohl around my eyes. Exiting the stall, I saw a group of young women milling by the bathroom mirror, talking excitedly about the evening.

'Excuse me,' I said as I politely pushed through to wash my hands.

'You're Jhanvi!' one of the girls said. 'Please! You must take a picture with us!' She thrust her cell phone forward as the other girls gathered around. I nodded my head, not quite ready to commit myself to words for fear of tears pushing through again.

'You can do this, Jhanvi,' I told myself as I left the ladies' room. For the remainder of the night, I busied myself down in the crowd, eventually making my way back up to Puneet, who was looking sorry for himself.

'This music is hurting my head,' he muttered like a belligerent toddler. The coffee and water had begun to take effect; I could see that a hangover was beginning to set in.

'The music is no different to what it was when you were drunk and sticking your tongue into another woman's mouth,' I shot back. I had already told the club manager that we were leaving. 'Get up, let's go,' I hissed at him. He pulled himself off the couch, steadier on his feet this time. The taxi drive back to his apartment was silent; I was not ready to talk to him about what had transpired on our first big night out together. Climbing the stairs to his one-bedroom apartment, we remained silent. It was only once we were inside that either one of us decided to speak.

'You know my history,' I began the conversation I could see he was trying to avoid. 'What Gaurav did to me almost broke me, and now you, Puneet.'

'I'm drunk, Jhanvi, and was even more drunk then,' he whined. His eyes were bloodshot, and I thought I saw regret somewhere behind the raging hangover that was taking control of him. I let it slide, not interested in a rehash of the drama caused by Gaurav's infidelity.

'Never again, Puneet,' I whispered, before walking out.

Now, as I find myself climbing those stairs to his apartment again, my thoughts have returned to that night and the following morning. I should have been more assertive, set the boundaries in our relationship. Instead, I had avoided the conflict and accepted his excuses. I thought our relationship had been fine since that evening, that his temporary lapse in judgement had brought us closer together. This morning though, I received a text from a friend.

'I'm sorry, Jhanvi,' it said.

Attached was a photographic explanation of the apology. A photograph of what my friend had seen when she was out the previous night. It was blurry, but it clearly showed Puneet with another woman. The kiss could not be passed off as anything other than romantic. At that moment, I was sure my heart shattered; the pain in my chest, the tightness in my throat and the flood of tears could not mean anything other than that. And, as it shattered, my mind sprang into action, trying desperately to pick up the fragments of my heart and glue them back to what they were. I told myself this wasn't my fault; that, although I was guarded, I had given him enough of my heart for him to break it, destroying my commitment to him.

Knocking on the door, I took a deep breath and closed my eyes to find my inner strength for the conversation that was about to take place, willing the jagged pieces of my heart to remain glued in their fragile state. I kept my eyes closed and my breath held until Puneet opened the door.

'Jhanvi, my darling, come in. You're looking gorgeous as always,' he said as he leaned forward to kiss me. I turned my face, presenting my cheek to him. His lips brushed my skin and my stomach churned, thoughts of the picture preventing me from reciprocating. How could he stand there and pretend he cared even after what he had done?

'Puneet, we have to talk,' ' I said curtly. The colour drained from his face. And there, at that moment, I knew it was the end for good. His expression read only of guilt for being caught, rather than the actions themselves. This conversation was going to be painful, I thought. And I was right. The conversation did not go well; he accused me of being detached and not being present in our relationship. I could not accept his explanation a second time. In the heat of the argument, it transpired that this was not the second woman he had cheated with; there had been many more. I felt sick and needed to escape. I left after collecting the few belongings I had at his house, slamming the door behind me.

I ran down the stairs, swallowing down the tears. I had no energy left to fight; this was another ruined relationship, filled with manipulation and lies. I needed to focus on my career, needed to formulate a plan to explain why yet another boyfriend was missing from my profile. I wondered whether my career was the reason nobody was able to love me, or whether I truly was as distant as they kept telling me. I don't see myself as unlovable, I think I am capable of accepting the love of others, but somehow, they all had the same excuse. It was always me; they never took responsibility.

I breathed deeply as I made my way towards the bus stop. I wouldn't allow myself to be vulnerable. Not now. Not because of a man. Sitting at the bus stop, I pulled my phone out of my bag and began to scroll through my notifications. A comment caught my eye: *'You are so beautiful, I wish I had your life,'* it read. I rolled my eyes and thought, 'If only you knew.'

2

ASHRAY

My alarm was set for two hours before I would normally wake up. When it went off, I rolled over; eyes closed, I swiped left, knowing that it would give me the extra ten minutes I needed to pull myself out of my deep sleep. I made a mental note to make sure the sound of the alarm going off wouldn't get loud enough to wake my mother. I had told her the previous night, while I ironed my shirt, that it was not necessary to get up early with me. I knew she probably would anyway. Lying in bed now, I reflected on my life since I had come to live with her.

'Akshita' means permanent, and at the time that I came to live with her, I needed someone permanent and steadfast in my life. I was a baby when I was left on the steps of an orphanage in Mumbai. I never knew my parents or whoever it was who left me there; I was never allowed to grieve for the loss of my parents. I was an orphanage child, that was my life. In a cruel twist of fate, it turned out that I was a particularly soft child, one that needed a lot of love and attention. This was not readily available at the orphanage. There were too many of us, and all too often it was the older kids, the funnier kids or the more assertive ones that drew the attention of our caregivers.

I do not remember when Akshita came into my life, but she told me she used to visit the orphanage often from when I was very young. What I do remember is that she was beautiful; kind brown eyes followed me while I played, and we would often spend time together during her visits. She was widowed and visited the orphanage to fill her life with the love of children. We formed a bond which felt to me to be unbreakable. She soothed my childlike mind and brought out a light in me that

I didn't know existed. But every time she left, panic consumed me. A panic that gnawed at me, telling me that she would never come back. At that young age, I already felt things far too strongly. In the orphanage, those feelings were fear. Fear of the other children, fear of being hurt and taunted, and fear of never seeing the beautiful woman who showered me with love again.

She stayed true to her name though, and by the time I was five, she had adopted me, and Akshita was never to be called by her name again, at least not by me. She was now my Maa, and she was as attentive to my needs at home as she was in the orphanage. I always had a loving ear to speak to, with an abundance of advice being returned by her. Together we worked through my internal pain and fears. She was never impatient, instead always lovingly soothing me when the fear welled up inside me that she wouldn't be standing at the school gates waiting for me at the end of the day.

Eventually, the fear and anxiety subsided. She doted on me; I loved her for it.

The previous night, she had fought with me when I wanted to iron my shirt, insisting that I didn't need to do it; she was quite capable.

'Maa, I am grown now. I must do these things by myself,' I told her with nothing but love in my eyes. She responded with a laugh, but pride filled her own eyes.

'Tomorrow, Ashray, you must be yourself. Show them you are very capable of doing this job. You are listening?' she said to me, full of advice as always.

'Yes, Maa.' I smiled at her, only showing her the confidence in me, knowing there was no point in arguing with her.

'You will be smart, presentable, full of knowledge, but be friendly too. They must know you can work well with your colleagues. Yes?' she added.

I put my shirt on a hanger, admiring my handiwork before kissing her on the forehead and saying goodnight. I smiled to myself as I made my way to bed; our relationship was the best thing I had in my life, and we spent plenty of time giving each other love and receiving it from the other.

'Don't forget your Maa when you are an important manager in the company, Ashray,' she called after me.

I let out a loud laugh and called back, 'Never, Maa. You will have a cottage on my property to grow old in.'

My alarm went off for a second time. I switched it off and swung my legs out of bed. 'Today will be a good day,' I told myself before making my way into the bathroom quietly. It was still early, and after many years of dragging my lazy teenage self out of bed, my mother deserved the rest.

Switching on the tap, I splashed cold water on my face to wake up. Looking in the mirror, I examined my face. I needed to shave. I filled the sink with warm water and began the ritual of removing my facial hair. Once I was more established in my position, I would allow myself a five o'clock shadow, but today, I had to make the best impression. As I swept the razor over my face, I took in my features. I liked to imagine that I looked like my father, but had my mother's eyes. It was strange for me to not have an idea of my real identity. Who did I belong to before Maa? At times, I felt detached, but Maa was always there to pull me back and remind me that love didn't require blood.

'Definitely my mother's eyes,' I said as I examined my handiwork in the mirror. Satisfied that I was cleanly shaved, I dried my face off and switched on the shower. Steam filled the room, as I allowed the hot water to wash off the last of my grogginess. Out of the shower, I examined myself in the mirror once more; the unruly, thick, black hair was mocking my perfectly shaved face. I placed coconut oil in my hands, and rubbed them together vigorously to warm the waxy substance up before smoothing it through my hair. I washed my hands and combed my hair into its usual style. I took another quick look in the mirror. 'Looking sharp,' I told my reflection.

Back in my bedroom, I dressed in the black suit Maa had bought me for my twenty-fifth birthday. The neatly ironed light blue shirt went perfectly with it. Staring at my ties, I decided on the more subtle dark blue tie to bring my look together. There would be time for flamingos and cartoon characters later on. I bent down to tie the laces on my worn leather shoes. Standing up, I examined myself in the mirror and brushed out the creases that had formed from bending over.

I made my way through the house and into the kitchen. Sitting at the table was Maa; she was still in her nightgown, her long black hair, streaked with reds and greys, cascaded down her back. She was reading yesterday's newspaper and sipping on some tea; tea had been prepared for me as well. Next to the mug was a bowl of Mysore bonda.

'Good morning, beta,' she said. 'Let me look at you.' She gestured for me to come closer for inspection.

'Morning, Maa,' I replied, walking up to her.

'Very handsome, my boy. Sit. Have your tea and eat.' She gestured towards the place I had sat since I was a child.

'Maa, you didn't need to do this,' I said, before sitting down at the table.

'You cannot go to a big interview with no food in your belly. Sit. Eat,' she said before returning to her newspaper. I smiled; I loved this woman so much. She was the reason I was interviewing for this job today—I wanted to give her a better life. To repay her for everything she had done for me. I sipped my tea and took a bite of a bonda.

'Anything interesting?' I asked her, pointing to the newspaper she was reading.

She turned the page before answering. 'I only look at the advertisements in these things, Ashray. The media only reports on sadness and heartache. I see these things every day when I walk to the market, and I do not need to read about them also.' She folded the newspaper. Picking up her teacup, she turned her attention to me.

'You have your CV and copies of your degree and certificates?' she asked.

'Yes, Maa,' I replied, getting up to put my dishes in the kitchen sink.

'Good. You can do this, Ashray,' she said; her eyes, filled with love and faith, met mine.

I kissed her on the cheek and, picking up my old leather briefcase, walked out the door to catch a bus.

On the bus, I reflected on how hard my Maa had worked to ensure that I was able to get the qualifications I needed to be successful. She was a woman who had so little but gave so much. I strived for success, not just for me, but to repay her for all she had done for me.

There are moments of realisation in our lives that force us to make decisions about our future. Good decisions. But even the good ones can be tough when you fear letting down people who have been good to you. I knew my self-worth though; well, I thought I did; and I knew my first job was a good one. But it didn't offer me growth or development in the company. When I finished my studies, I had applied for a position in sales and marketing at my current company. A few years later, there I was, turned down for a promotion, and my requests for a salary increase declined.

Getting off the bus, the humid Mumbai air filled my lungs. People walked with purpose, only occasionally stopping to sidestep someone asking for money. I made my way to the office block without much hassle; earlier in the week, I had taken the bus here to make sure I would not get lost. The building was new, and the huge glass windows reflected the August sun. I straightened my tie and walked into the building.

'I am here to interview at BusinessForward,' I said, leaning against the security desk. The guard didn't look up from his phone. He silently pointed at the book in front of me to sign in, which I did.

When I put the pen down, he muttered, 'Fourth floor.'

I walked towards the elevator, taking in the building.

BusinessForward occupied the fourth and fifth floors of the building. They were the leading consultancy agency in India, and their offices were a display of their success. Entering the office, I was very aware that this interview could change my life for the better. I walked up to the reception and introduced myself. I was given a form to fill in, and then led to the waiting room. The room was stark; white walls were decorated with oversized pictures of good-looking people shaking hands and looking satisfied with the service they had received. Four other candidates in suits were already there, filling in forms; none of them looked up to greet me as I sat down.

'Ashray?' a voice called out.

I looked up and saw a formally dressed, petite woman. 'That's me,' I said and smiled, determined to make a good impression from the start.

'Vihaan will see you now,' she said and led me from the room to the elevator. We rode the elevator up one floor before getting out and making our way down a passage to an office encased in glass. The woman opened the door, motioning for me to enter, before closing the door behind me.

'Vihaan Ahuja, director of BusinessForward,' the man behind the desk said while rising and offering a hand. 'Please. Have a seat.'

3
JHANVI

The bus stop was busy with people making their way home. It was late afternoon by the time I had plucked up the courage to confront Puneet. If I could have avoided the argument altogether, deleted him from my life, I would have. I didn't want to fight with him; I just wanted what little was left at his apartment and to leave, to forget he ever existed and that he had the power to hurt me as deeply as he had. But I wish I had chosen a different time, perhaps late at night when the buses would be emptier, and the streets would be filled with people who carried as much sorrow as I did in my heart.

I skipped two buses that would have taken me home, preferring to get lost in my phone while I tried to compose myself, occasionally fighting back tears. I considered removing all the photos of Puneet from my social media account while I sat there, but I wasn't ready for the onslaught of questions my followers would have. Perhaps I should post new pictures as usual, and nobody would notice the old ones disappearing from my feed? It would, at least, buy me some time to heal my heart.

A comment popped up on my feed, and I recognised the name. Clicking on it, I was directed to the commenters page. Happy faces smiled back at me; my own heart ached. Was I so difficult to love? I scrolled down, the void inside me aching to be filled. I clicked on the picture of the commenter—it was taken on her wedding day, and brightly coloured sarees filled the screen. 'They look truly happy with each other,' I whispered to myself.

I quickly clicked on another profile. I didn't want to get caught up in a couple's happiness now. Not while my heart was breaking. The person I viewed next was popular, far more popular than me, but I noticed that there was no boyfriend on her account. All her pictures were with her friends, carefully curated to show that she was strong and independent. Clicking back to my account, I scrolled quickly through my feed. Skipping over anything that reminded me of Puneet, I focused on my content; looking at my follower count and checking my page views, I continued to filter through my feed.

'You don't need a man, Jhanvi,' I told myself. 'You have a good follower count; you are already invited to some great events. You can be just as famous as these other women.' Locking my phone and putting it in my bag, I decided to walk to the market. With new clarity and a destination in mind, I pushed my way through the crowds. The market was filled with people haggling for the best possible price. The day's rubbish and offcuts littered the pavement. Street children rummaged through discarded items, hoping to pick up something they could sell or swap for something to eat.

A group of tourists walked past, directed by an Indian woman dressed in a bright red salwar kameez. Local traders tried desperately to push their wares on the tourists. A woman with blonde hair dug into her pocket and handed a doe-eyed child some money. The child slunk into the crowd before being noticed by other children begging on the street; I was sure she would go straight back to her mother to hand her the money. I reflected on my childhood, how I was spared all of this heartache. I had a good upbringing, my father and mother were always present, they worked hard to provide for me, and if I was honest, I never needed anything from them. Money had not come easy, but it was never scarce either. I don't remember much about those early years, other than that I was a loner who enjoyed playing by myself. I did not have a sibling, and as an only child, I was often only in adult company. I looked very much like my mother, and when I attended high school, boys began to notice me. I was frequently told how beautiful I was; inevitably, I found my way to social media, where my following began to grow from school friends to a larger audience.

But as my online presence grew, the distance between my parents and me also grew. They were born in a different generation, one where marriages were strictly arranged and no cell phones existed, let alone social media.

'Life is out there, Jhanvi,' my father would say, when I sat cooped up in my room, scrolling through profiles for hours. 'Why don't you go out and make some friends? Try and socialise a little bit?' I would inevitably roll my eyes and make empty promises to spend more time at friends' houses. He didn't understand that, these days, you made friends online.

For me, the pressure to be perfect was very real. To my parents, I was already perfect. It became more and more difficult for me to communicate to them the strains I was under. Eventually, I gave up altogether, preferring to hide behind the LCD screen in my hand.

'Excuse me,' a young girl said, standing in front of me. 'Are you her?' The girl, fifteen or sixteen years old, pointed at her phone. The screen was filled with small squares of me smiling outside designer stores with Puneet's arm around me.

'Yes. Would you like a selfie together?' I asked. I knew I didn't look my best, but consoled myself that the girl probably didn't have a very large following.

'Yes, please!' she squealed. 'My friend and I think you are so beautiful. We saw you at The Gateway, but you were busy with your boyfriend. Puneet? If you look in the background there, you will see us!'

I smiled, desperately wanting to tell these girls that my life was not as perfect as it appeared. Instead, I pulled them in close, directing them on how to place their chin and which was the right way to stand to capitalise on the afternoon sun. The girls lapped up my advice, promising to use it every time they took a photo, before hugging me and walking away, heads down as they watched their screens for likes.

Shaking off the dark thoughts that had begun to cloud my mind again, I set off to where I had been heading before the girls interrupted me. In front of me lay stalls of flowers in every colour imaginable. Because I was wearing blue, I found a stall with predominantly yellow flowers and pulled my phone out of my bag. Hitting the camera icon, I fixed my hair. Face angled, hair perfect, I took ten shots before scrolling through them to see if any of my captures were workable. I settled on one shot; I had a slight smile, and the sun caught my dark eyes perfectly and created a halo above my brown hair. 'I'll have to filter this,' I thought. Putting my phone back in my bag, I made my way back to the bus stop.

The bus was crowded. People were standing near the door, fighting for space, worried that they would not have enough time to get off at their next stop. I looked towards the back of the bus; a man in a black suit was sitting there. His legs were spread, and he was taking up far more space than he should have been doing. I pushed my way through the crowd, trying to keep my balance as the bus stopped and started through the traffic. I sat down forcefully, pushing the man's legs back out of my space. His face was buried deep in some documentation, and he didn't respond. Taking out my phone, I opened my usual filter app. Uploading the picture I took at the flower market, I started playing with its adjustments; face thinner, lights amplified, skin flawless. When I was satisfied with the results, I uploaded it to my account. Instantly, my screen begins to fill up with hearts. I sighed; at least my followers were loyal.

Locking the screen, I allowed myself to think about Puneet; about how I could have been so preoccupied that I did not see he was cheating on me. He admitted to six women, and it was probably more, I thought. The familiar lump in my throat returned. My mind was at war with my instincts, to let go of the tirade of emotions pent up inside me. I turned my phone back over and put in my password. More than one thousand likes in five minutes. This could be quite a distraction, I thought to myself.

Looking up, I noticed how people were pushing and shoving for space. I remembered how, as a child, I would take the bus with my parents. I would always end up squashed between the two of them, probably to stop me from getting lost or being pulled out of the bus by the departing crowds.

'Stand close, Jhanvi, don't let go of my hand,' my mom used to say before we would get on the bus. I hated the bus but craved the physical touch of my parents, and in those moments, I would use the crowds as an excuse to nestle in close to them. I wondered if I should let my parents know that my latest relationship wouldn't end in marriage. This would be yet another disappointment in a long line of disappointments for them.

Quickly, I decided against telling my parents anything. Trying to explain my life and why I could not forgive Puneet just wasn't worth the aggravation.

The man in the suit next to me opened his briefcase to put his papers away; one paper drifted to the floor of the bus. I caught the name on the top right corner, BusinessForward, before the suit picked it up and meticulously placed it back in his briefcase. He got up, clutched his bag to his chest, and pushed his way to the front of the bus before getting off and disappearing into the distance. I opened my phone again, knowing I had some time before I would have to push my way to the front. My post was doing well.

I scrolled through to my messages. Selecting Kavya, I typed a quick message. *'He says it's all my fault that he can't keep it in his pants.'*

An older woman sat down next to me, and I couldn't help but feel like my space was being invaded. I moved over slightly, trying to guard my privacy as much as I could. Three dots appeared on my screen. At least my friend was loyal.

4

ASHRAY

Hard work. Perseverance. These are things we can control, and with enough of it, success is inevitable. Or at least that is what we are told, and, in this instance, it certainly seemed to be true. Luck and being open to opportunities are, of course, a part of it, but without the hard work, without drive and perseverance, luck and opportunity mean nothing.

The interview went well, I mused as I waited for the bus home. I opened my phone and sent a quick text to Maa to let her know that I was on my way back, and that the company director had been really accommodating.

When my alarm had gone off that morning, I had mentally prepared myself for the full company board to grill me about my experience. Instead, I was welcomed by Vihaan, who came across more like a friend than the director of a massively successful company. We spoke briefly about my experience and time at college, but most of the conversation revolved around our personal lives and how Vihaan had worked his way up from poverty. His parents had sacrificed a lot to send him to college, and he had wanted to make sure that he could provide for them in their retirement and give them everything they couldn't have while he was growing up.

I identified with the man interviewing me; our values were similar, and I found myself opening up briefly about my time at the orphanage and how I wanted to provide for my Maa in her twilight years. By the time the woman from reception reappeared to say the next candidate was waiting for his interview, I felt that even if I did not get the job, I had made a friend who could guide me in the right direction.

Before I left the building, I was given a stack of papers to read through. I put them in my briefcase and walked towards the bus stop. I took this bus often and knew that the back seats were often empty because people did not like to push their way to the front of the bus when it was time to get off. When I got onto the bus, I made my way through the crowd gathered in the centre of the bus. At the back, two empty seats called me. I sat down and opened my briefcase, taking out the papers that were given to me. The first page was a brief overview of the company and where their offices were located globally. The second set of papers was an in-depth document explaining the company's values and what was expected of their sales and marketing staff. It was signed off by the head of human resources, Gautam Pillai.

I mentally patted myself on the back, telling myself that if I had the documents, the interview must have gone extremely well. I put my briefcase between my open legs, steadying myself against the swaying of the bus, and started reading the documentation. At the third stop, a woman in blue pushed her way to the back and sat next to me, pulling my attention away from the document I was reading. I picked up my briefcase to put the papers away, deciding that I would walk the two stops rather than be interrupted again.

The woman looked like she had been crying; her dark brown eyes were filled with sadness, and her face was buried in her phone. Distracted, I dropped a paper; she didn't move, refusing to acknowledge my existence. Normally, a woman's rejection would send me into a downward spiral of self-loathing, but today was a good day, and I was certain that my future was looking a lot brighter than it was yesterday when I was on the commute home. I put the papers in my briefcase, making sure to keep the page I was reading on top of the pile. Clutching my bag to my chest, I pushed forward through the crowd.

It was threatening to rain; the monsoon had been mild this year, but the evenings still brought heavy downpours. I silently cursed myself for getting off the bus too early; I did not want to get caught in a downpour wearing my best suit. I walked fast, weaving past other people on their way home, stopping only momentarily to check if Maa had replied to my message. Unlocking my phone, I saw a message waiting for me. *'Bring me a paper, please. Thank you, son.'*

I decided to pick up a newspaper when I was closer to the apartment block. It would be pointless now, if the rain broke. As I made my way through the crowds, I replayed the interview in my head; I was sure I had the job, but didn't want to be too confident. Stopping at the local shop, I grabbed a newspaper for Maa. By the time I reached the stairs to my apartment, the first drops had begun to fall. I smiled. 'A good day indeed,' I said out loud. Opening the door to our apartment, the smell of samosas and dal greeted me, filtering through from the kitchen. Dropping my keys in the ceramic pot at the door before loosening my tie and hanging it by the door, alongside my jacket, I walked into the kitchen.

'Hello, Maa,' I said and grinned. 'Why am I being spoiled with my favourite food tonight?'

She turned and eyed me before returning my smile. 'So, your interview was good then,' she said. 'I told you to be yourself, and you will get the job. This is a good celebration, don't you think?'

I lifted my arms in defeat.

'Hang on! The interview was good, but they haven't given me the job yet.'

'Come, sit,' Maa said, motioning for me to sit at the kitchen table. 'We'll eat and talk about it, and then we will decide if you have the job, yes?'

Defeated, I sat down as she placed the dishes down on the table for dinner. I looked at my mother and love filled my heart.

In my darker times, I allowed myself to think about what life would be without this woman in it, and whether I would have been given these opportunities if I had lived my entire life in the orphanage.

'Now tell me,' she said as she spooned some food onto my plate. 'How did it go?'

Dinner was filled with conversations around the interview, of how Vihaan was now providing for his parents, and how I wanted to do the same for her. I told her what my position would be, making sure to tie in how my degree benefited the job. She listened to me intently, offering the occasional words of encouragement. When I was finished eating, she cleared the dishes and put a cup of tea in front of me. I began telling her about the company's global presence and how it meant that the opportunities for growth were great. She nodded in agreement, even if she didn't fully understand what I was talking about, and after our tea, she told me that she was proud of me but was tired. Kissing me on the forehead, she walked through to wash up for the evening.

I sat at the kitchen table, excited and anxious. I listened to the familiar sounds of my Maa completing her nightly routine, waiting until she was in bed so that I would not disturb her. Then I pulled out my laptop and switched it on. The screen turned blue; 'Welcome back' flashed on the screen before the half-circle began its usual clockwise turn. A picture of Maa and me came up on my dashboard; I clicked on the icon to open my email. Almost immediately, in bold, a message popped up from Gautam Pillai. The subject glared at me: *Interview BusinessForward today*

I took a deep breath and clicked on the email, my eyes closed tightly, knowing that when I opened them again, my life could potentially change, forever.

5
JHANVI

The phone screen lit up in my hand, startling me. I had been lost in my thoughts. It was Kavya who had sent me the message about Puneet that morning. She always had my best interests at heart, and for a long time she had suspected that Puneet was being unfaithful. She tried to prepare me for the inevitable, but she also knew that you could never be fully prepared for this kind of betrayal. She had not followed Puneet the night before; she was out with another group of friends, enjoying the night scene and drinking coffee, when the slimebag walked past them with his arm around another woman's waist. Knowing it would take some convincing, she had snapped a photo to send to me. She didn't want me to agonise about it all night, though, so she waited until morning to drop the bombshell.

We had grown up together, Kavya and I, having met so far back that neither of us could remember when it was exactly. Kavya was the closest I had ever come to having a sister, and when she told me she was moving to Mumbai, my heart was torn apart. We had spoken about it all through high school, planned and dreamed about a future in a city that would cater to both our dreams. She wanted to be an interior designer, so I knew that Mumbai was the obvious choice for her. A place where she could study and get work that would put her talents to use. I tried, really I did, to live without her steadfast, constant presence in my life, but somehow my existence seemed empty without her.

I opened the message from her.

'*Sorry, my friend, I didn't want to break your heart, but he doesn't deserve you, you know,*' it read.

I did know that, but you know how it is? Those questions you ask yourself: Could I have done better? What did I do to deserve this? Why am I unlovable?

I typed a message back.

'He has been doing this for months. I should be the one to say sorry for not believing you.'

I opened my social media account again and noticed that my like count was not going up as quickly as when I first posted. Quickly, I added hashtags to my comments section, being careful to put some in that insinuated I was newly broken up, but still looking fabulous and unbreakable. Another message pinged through from Kavya. *'You up for a cup of coffee?'*

Honestly, I just wanted to get home, to wash the day off of me and begin my new social media strategy. I typed out a message and hit reply: *'Almost home, catch up tomorrow.'*

I locked my phone and put it in my bag, clutching it to my chest. I stared at the crowd in front of me. I allowed myself to reflect on the confrontation that had happened a few hours earlier.

'You are never available, Jhanvi! How am I supposed to have a relationship with a woman who can't even talk about how she feels?'

'Perhaps I am, but seeing my boyfriend kissing another woman doesn't exactly inspire me to be emotionally available,' I shouted back. His first public betrayal had forced me to guard my heart; I had chosen what to share with him and what not to share with him after that, keeping him away from anything that revolved around my social media life. I attended gatherings without him and only included him in pictures where we were alone. Behind the scenes, though, I truly felt our relationship was better than it ever was. Puneet seemed attentive to my needs and keenly participated in any conversation we had.

When I had first confronted him earlier that day, he tried to deny any wrongdoing. Showing him the picture threw him into a rage. He had shouted and accused me of following him. I did not say much; instead, I had stood and listened to his poor excuses. I had already formulated my questions in my head, and I was waiting for an opening to ask them. When he told me that it was my fault, I snapped. He snapped back, telling me this was the most passion I had ever shown in our entire relationship. Wounded, I retreated to his bedroom, grabbing the few items of clothing I kept in his top drawer. He punched the wall as I made my way to the door, spitting at me that I was so uninvolved I didn't even realise he had been fooling around for months now. Slamming the door behind me, I vowed I wouldn't forgive him this time; wouldn't beg him for his affection.

Thinking back to my teenage years, I wondered if my detachment from my parents affected my relationships with men. My parents love me, I know this, but I learned that they did not understand me. Rather than argue my point and cause conflict, I locked my emotions away. I craved their affection, wished that I could reach out and hug my mother and ask her about all the emotions that were being caused by male affection. My mother often made me a cup of tea when I was at my lowest; we would sit in the kitchen together, my mom giving me a knowing look, but there was never any acknowledgement of anyone's feelings.

When I left school, my parents wanted me to go to college. With my budding social media career, I decided I would attend, but only for the parties and photo opportunities. I failed twice and was forced to drop out in the second year. My father was bitterly disappointed, I saw it in his eyes, but again, no words were spoken. By the time I dropped out of college, my online presence was making me enough money to survive; not enough to live extravagantly, but enough to pack my bags and move from our home in Delhi to Mumbai. My mom began a discussion the day before I moved, but when I pushed back, my mother agreed reluctantly.

Arriving in Mumbai, I moved in with Kavya for a month before finding my own apartment. I spent my days moving between various tourist spots, trying to fit in as much time as I could for my boyfriend and friends. Every Sunday, I called my parents to tell them I was all right.

The bus slowed down, snapping me back to the present. I looked out of the window, and saw that it had begun to rain heavily. I knew I would be drenched before I reached my front door. A familiar pain pressed against my chest. Swallowing hard, I stood up and slid between people, trying to push my way to the door. At the next stop, I got off into the torrential rain. While running through the downpour to get home, my pain became unbearable. I stopped to breathe. Lifting my head upwards, I let the pain go. Tears rolled down my face, disguised by the rain, and I let them fall. I walked the remaining distance to my apartment building slowly, allowing myself to release the pain inside me. Today I would mourn; tomorrow, Puneet would be nothing but a memory.

A few minutes later, I entered my apartment. It was silent; it always was. Walking into my living room, I removed my wet clothing. I walked into the kitchen and heated some water. I spooned loose tea into the teapot and poured the hot water in before going through to the bedroom. I pulled out a tracksuit from my closet and slipped it on. I switched on the bathroom light and opened the tap until the water was hot, too hot, and washed the grime of the bus off my face. Opening the bathroom cabinet, I removed a pack of makeup wipes, pulled one from the packet, and wiped the makeup from my face. Dark brown eyes stared back at me; they looked sad and not at all determined, which is not what I wanted. Blinking hard, I wiped my mascara off and then took a deep breath. I had to keep moving forward. 'You can do this, Jhanvi. You don't need him.'

Making my way back to the kitchen, I poured the tea through a strainer, sat on my couch and unlocked my phone. A message was waiting for me from Kavya. I didn't read it. Instead, I opened my account and went to the most popular person I followed. Pen and paper in hand, I scrolled through the feed, making notes on what pictures and captions had generated the most likes.

'Tomorrow,' I thought.

6

ASHRAY

I opened my eyes, and I began to read the email out loud.

Good evening, Ashray,

I have received feedback from our BusinessForward director regarding your application and interview for the position of sales and marketing consultant. I am pleased to tell you that the company found you well suited for the role and believes you will fit in with BusinessForward's culture. Please get in touch with me to discuss the details of the offer further.

Congratulations!

Gautam

By the time I had reached the second to last sentence, I was up from the table, air-punching and dancing around. Realising Maa was asleep not far from the kitchen, I covered my mouth guiltily before sitting down and hitting reply.

Good evening, Gautam.

Thank you for your e-mail. I appreciate the offer and look forward to working at BusinessForward. I am available on Monday, should you wish to arrange a meeting to finalise the offer.

Many thanks,

Ashray

I hit send and closed my laptop screen, not bothering to shut it down the correct way. I packed my laptop back in its bag, switched off the kitchen light, and made my way to the bathroom. Switching on the bathroom light, I turned the nozzle on the shower. Removing my suit trousers, I folded them neatly and placed them at the door before removing the rest of my clothes and putting them in the laundry basket.

I got into the shower, smiling. Perhaps this was the start of everything new in my life. Maybe I would find a woman who would settle down with me now, someone who would accept my mother as a part of our home. I felt that my dreams were almost within reach. I also knew that dreams were one thing— that you needed to find your purpose, believe ardently and your dreams would come true. But the truth is, those people who are successful, those who actually manage to achieve what they set out to do? Those are the people who get up every day and work hard, work persistently, to ensure that they surpass those who continue to only dream.

I got out of the shower, dried myself, and wrapped the towel around my waist. I did a little dance before leaving the bathroom, folded trousers in hand.

In my bedroom, I hung my trousers up, making a note to fetch my jacket and tie from the coat rack in the morning. Putting on a white t-shirt and a pair of track pants, I grabbed my journal and opened it to a blank page. I had begun keeping a journal a few years after I moved in with Maa, not only as a way to cope with my feelings, but as a way to keep my memories with her alive. Throughout my teen years, I wrote down all my victories and achievements, so that whenever I felt I had failed or couldn't achieve something, I could look back and motivate myself. Maa found the journal once; I knew this because it had moved from its original position. I didn't mind that she had read it. I never had anything negative to say about her anyway. Tonight, I penned down the details of my interview, how smart I looked when I left the house this morning, and how I managed to open up to the director of the company. I ended the entry with a copy of the email I had received from Gautam.

Closing the journal, I lay back on my bed and stared at the ceiling. The next day was a Saturday; I could work on my resignation letter. But first, I would go to the market in the morning and buy Maa a bunch of flowers to celebrate my new job. I closed my eyes, allowing thoughts of a perfect home to fill my mind; a place where Maa could grow old, happy and surrounded by grandchildren. Sleep enveloped me.

On Saturday morning, I got up early, knowing that Maa would sleep in after the previous morning's early start. I walked briskly down the main street until I reached the flower-seller by the corner. Grabbing a bunch of flowers and a newspaper, I paid the vendor and made my way back home. Opening the front door, I took my shoes off and walked through to the kitchen to find a vase to put the flowers in. The room filled with the fragrance of the flowers. I put the kettle on the stove and lit the gas. In the background, I heard Maa moving around. I must have woken her with the sound of the front door closing. The kettle whistled, and I began preparing our morning tea. I turned around to see her walk into the kitchen.

'Good morning, Maa.' I was unable to contain the excitement in my voice. 'Come. Sit. I have made you some tea. Here is your newspaper,' I said with a smile.

Maa smiled back at me, taking in the flowers, tea and my mood. 'Well, either you have received some very good news about your job, or you have found a nice young girl at the shop this morning,' she joked.

'I got the job, Maa!' I walked around to her side of the table and, bending down, I threw my arms around her. 'This is it! This is the beginning of our lives, Maa,' I said with a wide smile, squeezing her tightly.

She smiled proudly back at me. 'I knew you would get it, my boy. I am so proud of how far you have come.'

We sat around the table drinking tea and discussing the future. Maa offered her advice on how I should approach my resignation letter, reminding me that I should not burn bridges; she had raised me better than that, after all. An hour later, I stood up, telling her to get dressed while I typed out a rough draft of my resignation. Today, I wanted to spend time with her; I would take her to the flower market. I knew this was one of her favourite places to spend the day. I opened my laptop, and the screen instantly came to life. I berated myself for not shutting it down properly last night. An email had come in from Gautam, confirming a meeting for Monday afternoon. I typed a quick response and got down to putting together my resignation letter. By the time I was done, Maa was ready. Being careful to save the document and shut down correctly this time, I put my laptop away. We left the apartment together, arm in arm.

7

JHANVI

It's expected of human beings to cope, to somehow move on from an unimaginable tragedy. When an animal loses its friend, its life partner, we justify their behaviour, their inability to eat or sleep and their incessant crying, telling others how bad we feel for them. How great their heartache must be. But people? People are expected to move on, seemingly unaffected by their grief. We expect that grief comes with an expiry date and that, after that date, everything should return to the way it was. People are expected to be unchanged and unbreakable. The truth is that grief is immeasurable, insurmountable at times, and life will never be the same again. You will be changed; it will never be the same again even if you choose to pretend you are unchanged.

I opened my eyes; it was ten in the morning and the sun was streaming through my bedroom window. I groaned and rolled over. Taking my phone off charge, I put the code in to unlock it. I opened my account—seventeen thousand likes and a few thousand comments. Scrolling through the comments, I noticed the young girl from the market the day before. I hit reply and typed a personalised response before getting out of bed and walking through to the bathroom. I washed my face and applied my makeup to look as natural as possible. Brushing my hair, I put the curling iron through the front sections before setting it with dry shampoo. I switched off the curling iron and returned to my bedroom, taking off my tracksuit top and choosing a champagne camisole. Slipping it on, I got back into bed, grabbing my phone on the way. I angled the camera until the light was exactly right, and took bursts of photos that

I could scroll through while I was having my morning tea. Climbing back out of bed, I opened Kavya's message from the night before and typed a quick response saying we could meet for coffee in an hour.

In the kitchen, I made myself a cup of green tea and opened my phone gallery. Scrolling through the photos I'd just taken, I chose one where I was smiling, the sun was hitting my face, and the sheets were pulled up to my chin. If I were one of my followers, I would believe that my life was perfect. I opened the filter app and used my usual face tuning tricks before posting it to my account with the caption *'newly single and loving it'*. Instantly, my screen began to fill with hearts.

I smiled as I sipped my tea. By the end of next month, I would reach half a million followers. I would finally be happy; I didn't need a man to validate me. Putting my cup in the sink, I walked back into my bedroom to be confronted with my unmade bed.

'Making your bed is the right way to start your day, Jhanvi,' my dad used to say. 'It means you have already completed one thing.'

Rolling my eyes, I began choosing the perfect outfit for a casual, late summer Saturday. Flipping through my double wardrobe, I eventually decided on a yellow shirt and a pair of flowing white pants. Slipping on a pair of yellow pumps, I opened my makeup bag and added a few finishing touches to go out. Looking at myself in the mirror, I nodded in approval. Grabbing my keys and a pair of oversized sunglasses, I walked out of my apartment. I was ready to start this new chapter in my life; no Puneet needed, just me.

I ignored the pain in my chest when the thought of living without him entered my head. Stepping outside and onto the sidewalk, I hailed a cab. Climbing into the cab, I opened my phone and typed out a message to let Kavya know that I was on my way. I gave the taxi driver the destination address, sat back and opened my camera. Placing it close to the taxi window, I hit record, creating the next lot of content.

A short taxi-drive through Mumbai traffic, and I was at my friend's apartment block. I rang the buzzer, and the door buzzed open. I opted to take the elevator, rather than risk sweating while I walked the stairs up to the fifth floor. Before I could knock, Kavya opened the door, toothbrush in hand. She hugged me and mumbled for me to sit down. A few moments later, she emerged from the bathroom and greeted me properly.

'I'll pour us some juice, tell me what happened,' she said.

I didn't want to talk about it, but I knew my friend would not let it go until she had all the details.

'He denied it to begin with, of course,' I began, trying to hide the sound of my voice breaking. 'That was before he called me shallow and detached and admitted he had been fooling around for months.'

Kavya shook her head. 'The man is a swine, Jhanvi. They're not all like that, I promise you.'

I wondered how my friend always seemed to know what I was thinking. 'This is the second time, Kavya. I am starting to think that they *are* all like that. Anyway, what are we doing today?' I tried to change the subject before my tears started to fall.

'I thought we could go and get a late lunch, have a girl's day out,' Kavya responded. 'Perhaps take in a few sights?'

I nodded my head absentmindedly while I scrolled through my comments, trying to calculate what percentage I had moved up with my followers. Kavya told me that she was going to finish getting ready before disappearing into her room. I continued scrolling through my comments, selecting the ones I would respond to with a personalised message, and trying to avoid the ones that said anything negative about me. Since my account had become popular, I noticed how people who chose to be negative always spoke about me in the third person, as if I wasn't the person behind the account. One of them, this morning, had commented on how I sleep with makeup on. I made a face as my thumb hovered over the delete comment button. Finally, I just closed the app, choosing to ignore the comment, and made a mental note to take more care when trying to get the natural look with makeup.

I walked through to Kavya's room to help her decide what to wear. I knew that she would still be standing in front of her wardrobe trying to decide which pair of torn jeans and old t-shirt she would wear.

'We will be here all day if you are left to decide what to wear on your own,' I joked, moving her away from the open cupboard. I looked through her clothes and chose a pair of ankle-length skinny jeans and a light salmon oversized shirt. Keeping in mind that we would do some walking today, I pulled out a pair of light pink sneakers and put them in front of Kavya.

'Here, put this on,' I said, walking out of the room, 'and tuck that shirt in loosely.'

Back in the living room, I rummaged through my bag, looking for one item in particular. Kavya walked in, her black hair tied in a messy bun on top of her head. I examined her; if we were going to take photos today, she would need to be on-trend as well. Moving towards her, I methodically folded the sleeves perfectly, so they stopped by her elbows. I slid on the gold cuff I had pulled out my bag moments earlier.

'You still got those oversized glasses I gave you?' I asked. Kavya nodded and grabbed them from the hall counter, examining herself in the full-length mirror at the end of the passage. She smiled in approval.

'You would think you do this for a living,' she said jokingly. 'I look fabulous for someone who is wearing five-year-old jeans and an ex's shirt.'

I giggled. I grabbed my bag from the couch and, after one last touch-up of my makeup, we left Kavya's house. In the elevator ride down, I took a picture of us smiling. I truly was happy at that moment. I wouldn't bother with filters this time; the lighting in the elevator was perfect. I hashtagged it #girlsdayout and pressed post. Outside in the hot summer sun, we walked arm in arm to our favourite neighbourhood restaurant. Our usual spot in the corner was free, and we ordered iced tea before Kavya brought the conversation back to what had happened with Puneet.

'I meant what I said, Jhanvi, not all men are the same. You shouldn't give up on love.' She looked deeply into my eyes, searching for some sign that I understood and believed her.

'This is the third long-term boyfriend I've had, Kavya, and two of them thought so little of me that they cheated. I am done with men for a long time. If you want to do something for me, keep me away from any man with chocolate skin and a set of abs, yeah?' I unlocked my phone to check how my post was doing; hearts filled my screen. I made a mental note—followers up by ten—before turning my attention to my inbox. Amongst all the fan mail and unsavoury photos of male body parts was a message from Burn Promotions. I opened it.

Jhanvi, we notice your account has the following that our brand needs. Burn Promotions would like to offer you two VIP tickets to the Goa Music Festival, all expenses paid, of course. DM me so we can make arrangements.

'Oh my gosh, Kavya, it's the Goa Music Festival next weekend!' I screamed with excitement. Kavya lifted her head from her phone, interest piqued. 'The promotions company is offering me two VIP tickets, all expenses paid. What do you say?'

Kavya let out a shriek before slinking back in her chair; the surrounding patrons scowled at us as we collapsed into fits of giggles.

'I will take that as a yes then. But I am choosing your outfits, this could be make or break for my career, and we need to look on-point,' I mocked.

Kavya nodded her head in approval before sticking her tongue out at me. I opened my messages and hit reply;

Thanks for your gracious offer. I would love to attend the Goa Music Festival this year and document it on my social media for you. Please let me know how to proceed.

Having paid our bill, we walked out of the restaurant, chattering about the following weekend and how this could be a turning point in my career. All thoughts of Puneet had been temporarily halted, replaced with dreams of grand careers and extravagant lifestyles, where we would live in a penthouse overlooking Mumbai.

8

ASHRAY

My alarm was set early for the first day of my new job at BusinessForward. I didn't want to be late. When I got out of bed, Maa was already up, and I could smell the familiar aroma of breakfast filtering through the house. I smiled; she was amazing. Opening my cupboard, I decided against the flamingo tie again; I still needed to make a good impression. Instead, I opted for a sensible green tie, a crisp white shirt and my blue suit. I completed my morning routine before walking into the kitchen.

Maa smiled and said, 'You look good, Ashray.'

'Thanks, Maa.' I leaned and kissed her on the head before sitting at my usual spot. I wolfed down breakfast; I hadn't realised I was that hungry. Standing up from the table, I placed my dishes in the sink before grabbing my briefcase to leave. This morning, I would take the early train to the BusinessForward office. I could not rely on the bus being on time.

Arriving at the station, I instantly regretted my decision. The train was crammed full of early morning commuters with the same idea I had. My stress levels rose as I walked the length of the carriage, trying to find an empty seat. A large man who had been snoring and grunting only moments before stood up abruptly and walked to the door, pushing past a young woman and her mother. Sitting down quickly, I smiled; thankfully, I would not be seated next to him for my journey. The woman sitting next to me smiled. Her face was warm; her eyes lined with kohl smiled as warmly as her mouth. I smiled back and opened my phone quickly so that I didn't look desperate for her attention. I put my phone back in my pocket and nervously tapped my briefcase, trying to distract myself.

'Hi. My name is Sakshi,' the woman said. I was grateful she didn't offer her hand to shake, my own hands were sweating profusely. I wondered how she could be smiling this early in the morning. Perhaps she too was starting a new job, like me.

'Hi,' I managed. 'I'm Ashray. Nice to meet you.'

Her mother rolled her eyes at her daughter.

'Well, Ashray. Why are you on the train this early in the morning?' she asked with a smile, ignoring her mother's displeasure.

I leaped at the opportunity to tell someone other than Maa about my new job and my plans for the future.

'I am starting a new job today as a marketing consultant at BusinessForward. They are this really big global company, which offers great opportunities for growth,' I added, hoping to impress her sighing mother. 'And you, Sakshi? What are you doing on the train this early?'

She smiled again. 'I am accompanying my mom to the hospital to see a specialist. They need to do some tests on her heart.' Her mother coughed, unimpressed that her daughter was sharing such intimate details with a stranger.

The journey was filled with conversations about my job and Sakshi's mother's health. By the time we reached her stop, I was hoping she would give me her number.

'It was really nice chatting with you, Ashray,' she said, beaming as she stood up. 'I hope your new job is everything you dreamed of.' Before she walked to the door, she turned back to me. 'Maybe we'll meet again. Wouldn't that be fortuitous?' Her mother rolled her eyes again, and ushered Sakshi from the train. And just like that, she was gone.

If it were any other day, I would have been upset, but nothing could dampen my spirits today. Soon enough, it was my stop. Hopping off the train, I pushed through the crowds. It was already hot, and I could feel the humidity in the air. The last thing I wanted was to get stuck in a downpour. Orienting myself, I walked towards the office. I was early. Very early. I planned on getting a coffee at the café on the lower level of the building and going through the documents the company had given to me on the day of the interview. Entering the building, a familiar voice greeted me.

'Ashray! Good to see my new employee is enthusiastic enough to get to work early.' It was Vihaan, standing at the counter of the café in his Armani suit, smiling. 'Coffee?'

'Yes please,' I said, digging into my trouser pocket for money. He waved his hand, dismissing my attempts to pay. The girl behind the counter handed us two paper cups. The smell of the coffee made me think it was what sophistication would smell like.

'Come,' he said and motioned towards the elevator, 'meet some of our other early birds.' In the elevator, I glanced as covertly as I could at what he was wearing. Suddenly, I became very aware of my worn shoes.

'Next month, you will be able to afford a new suit,' he said, as if he were reading my thoughts. 'The month after that, some new shoes and maybe a nice cologne.' I blushed, wondering if I smelled strange from the train ride here. 'If you apply yourself, in a few months you will be wearing everything new, but this,' he turned and tapped my old briefcase, 'this, you never replace, Ashray. We all need a reminder of where we came from. You understand?' I nodded my head enthusiastically, taking in what my mentor was saying.

The elevator doors opened and Vihaan ushered me through reception into the large open plan office. Pigeonhole desks lined with marketing plans were divided by small partitions. A telephone and flat-screen computer sat on top of each desk. Gathered around one desk were three men, all smartly dressed and laughing at something the seated man was saying. Vihaan gestured for me to follow him and then walked me over to the group.

'Guys, meet Ashray; he is our newest team member,' he said, motioning for me to step forward. 'Ashray this is Rishi, he is one of our top consultants. You will be shadowing him for your first week here. I am sure he will introduce you to the rest.' Rishi extended his hand and smiled. 'Rishi will take you through to human resources when they arrive. They'll give you your passwords so you can access the company system.' Vihaan shook my hand firmly before leaving for his own office.

'So, Ashray,' Rishi interrupted me as I was staring at Vihaan's retreating figure. 'He's quite the guy, huh?'

Embarrassed, I tried to make an excuse, but Rishi laughed it off, telling me that if I didn't at least admire Vihaan, there was something wrong with me.

The first week passed in a blur, learning about my new role and being integrated into the team. Rishi and I quickly became friends, spending lunchtime in the cafeteria below. I opened up to him about my dreams and aspirations while working at the company, and he assured me that they were definitely possible to achieve within this organisation. He took me under his wing, insisting on paying for lunches and early morning coffees. I told him about how I was left at an orphanage and how my Maa took me into her home.

He was a funny guy, the office clown, but he knew his job, and he was extremely good at it. By the third day, when he told me I didn't need his training, I glowed with confidence, knowing that I was in the right place.

On Friday, the end of my first week at BusinessForward, Rishi rolled his office chair out of his cubicle. Leaning back, he tapped me on the shoulder. I was deep in thought, examining a client's portfolio.

'Hey, Ashray, it's the Goa Music Festival this weekend. I wasn't going to go because all these clowns are too scared to be seen in public with me,' he said with a mock scowl, and laughed at Vijay in the cubicle behind us. 'What do you say? I have two tickets for the fest, and I have already paid for the accommodation.'

I opened my mouth to make an excuse. I didn't want to leave Maa alone for an entire weekend, even though I knew she would be angry at me for not going because of her.

'No, listen,' Rishi interrupted before I could say anything, 'I am not accepting no for an answer. So tonight, you go home, pack your bag, and I will meet you at the station for the late train to the airport. We'll catch the red-eye. It's on me.' I nodded, half excited, half in a panic. 'Great,' he said, wheeling his chair back into his cubicle.

I grabbed my phone and sent a quick text to Maa.

A friend has invited me away for the weekend, Maa. I am sorry, I couldn't refuse.

She replied instantly.

'Why are you apologising, Ashray? I am so happy you have a new friend.'

I smiled. I mentally prepared what I would take with me. By five that afternoon, Vihaan sent out an email saying we could leave early because it was a Friday. I took the train home, even though I knew it would be crowded. I was holding out hope that I would see Sakshi, but again, she was nowhere in the carriage.

9

JHANVI

The week before the music festival was spent deciding on our outfits; they had to be perfect. Big names were playing, and music celebrities were sure to be there. For the trip there, I chose a pair of torn jeans, a silver sequined bikini top and a loose-fitting denim button-up shirt. I finished the look with a flower head garland and a pair of big gold-hooped earrings. Kavya protested when I tried to dress her up, saying she would rather fly to Goa in a comfortable t-shirt and jeans.

Burn Promotions arranged for Kavya and me to be picked up in a town car on Saturday morning. In the car, a bottle of champagne awaited us. Opening the bottle, I giggled as I poured out the golden bubbly liquid into the glasses provided. Kavya shook her head, saying it was too early to drink. I downed her drink and my drink, one after the other, telling her to stop being a buzzkill. At the airport, I was surprised to find out that Burn Promotions was flying all of its influencers on a private chartered plane. I poked Kavya with an elbow; she didn't respond. Turning to her, I realised she was gawking at the plane open-mouthed. I laughed.

'Is this your life now, Jhanvi?' she said, wide-eyed. 'If I knew all these people were travelling with us on a private plane, I would've worn what you told me to.'

I linked my arm with hers and smiled broadly, the two glasses of champagne giving me courage and making me lightheaded. I gestured towards the plane. 'This is our life now, Kavya!' I said, laughing.

We climbed up the steps that lead into the small private jet. Inside, four other influencers sat waiting. On each seat was a care package that contained face products, Burn Promotion goods and snacks for the flight. Inside the package was another bag. I opened it, and inside, a small bottle of champagne stared at me. I put the bottle at the bottom of the bag and turned to speak to Kavya. She was sitting with her mouth open again, a look of dread on her face.

'Oh my god, what now, Kavya?'

She didn't say anything at first. Then, pulling herself out of her trance, she turned to me and said, 'Look, Jhanvi, this is not the end of the world. It's only an hour's flight, and then the bus ride to the hotel. I'm sure we can handle that.' Confused, I looked towards where she had been gazing moments earlier. At the entrance to the plane stood Gaurav; his latest conquest, scantily dressed, hanging from his arm.

'How the hell did that son of a bitch manage to get on the PR list?' I cursed loudly.

Kavya put her hand on my arm as Gaurav walked past and winked at me. The girl with him curled her nose up at me before turning to whisper to him. He took the seat behind me, which I knew was a passive-aggressive attempt at trying to intimidate me.

Leaning over my seat, he said, 'Hey Jhanvi, excuse my girlfriend's manners.' He emphasised the word girlfriend. 'She is a little jealous we will be spending the weekend together.'

Without turning around, I spat back, 'WE will not be doing anything together this weekend, Gaurav.' Turning to his girlfriend, I said, 'Remember to use protection with this one, darling. He likes to sleep around.' I slumped back into my chair as Kavya gawked at me.

The girlfriend protested loudly enough for Gaurav to try and protect his reputation, and he agreed to move to another seat. I reached into the gift bag and took out the bottle of champagne. I didn't know if they provided glasses; at that stage,

I didn't care. I opened it and downed the contents. Kavya looked at me, concern on her face. I ignored it and asked her if she was going to drink her bottle. She said no, but refused to allow me to drink anymore before we landed.

By the time the plane took off, I was buzzed and emotionally tired. I closed my eyes.

I was woken by Kavya when we landed. My head throbbed and my mouth was dry. I downed a glass of orange juice before we got off the plane, cursing myself for not taking pictures earlier. On the landing strip, I slipped on my sunglasses and convinced Kavya to take a picture of me with the plane in the background. My excuse was that I wanted a full body shot; the real reason was what she was wearing. To placate her, we took a selfie; I knew I would not post it online.

Waiting for us was a luxury tour bus and another care package with some sweet gin and premixed coolers tucked neatly into the backs of the seats in front of us. I would need this if I was going to survive the nearly two-hour trip to Vagator Beach, confined on a bus with Gaurav. The bus started, and loud music began pumping through the speakers. I pulled out my phone to post the photo of me in front of the private jet. Standing, I took another photo of the other influencers dancing in the aisle. I hadn't spoken to any of them, other than my run-in with Gaurav, but it made for a good shot. I hashtagged the original photo and posted it before sitting down and opening one of the coolers. Kavya looked at me.

'Do you really think that's a good idea, Jhanvi?'

'I don't know, Mom! Is it?' I mocked. She looked back at me, wounded.

'Look, Kavya, I'm not going to get drunk, but my head is pounding from the flight, and at least this will keep me relaxed enough to not argue with Gaurav.' She nodded, and I hugged her as an apology. I took another cooler out and offered it to her. Kavya accepted it reluctantly. We clinked our bottles together and smiled for another selfie.

The trip down to Vagator Beach was a blur. Kavya, still annoyed with me, stood up to speak to the other influencers on the bus. I sat sulking in my seat, occasionally shooting glares at Gaurav and his girlfriend. The gin coolers were working to keep my emotions under control though, and by the fourth one, I was up and dancing with the others. I should have been talking to those who had a higher follower count about their strategies, but my ego was too bruised to care at that stage. I took short videos of us dancing and the interior of the bus, and I took a photo of Gaurav and his girlfriend arguing because he was dancing with another girl. I thought about posting it to my stories and hashtagging it with something witty, but I decided it wasn't worth the drama I would have to endure over the weekend.

Disembarking, we were led to our accommodation, not too far from the main stage. Luxurious hotel rooms with an itinerary waited for us.

Kavya flopped down onto her bed. 'You should probably have a shower to sober up,' she commented. I couldn't argue, I was feeling lightheaded; I hadn't eaten, and I needed to make a good impression.

I switched the shower to as cold as it would go. Standing under the stream of water, I tried to wash all thoughts of Gaurav and Puneet away. Once I felt sufficiently sober, I hopped out of the shower and wrapped a big white fluffy towel around me. Looking at myself in the mirror, I smiled; surely this trip would be the start of something new. I walked back into the room. Kavya was sitting on the bed, scrolling through her phone. She looked up at me, staring hard, probably trying to ascertain if I was sober.

'Your post is doing well,' she said. I dived across the room onto her bed. She burst out laughing. I put my head on her lap while she showed me the photo. Twenty-three thousand likes in two-and-a-half hours. I reached out and tapped the heart button on her phone; twenty-three thousand and one.

'I'm sorry,' I whispered.

'I know,' she said, smoothing my hair away from my eyes. 'Come, get up now. It's time to play dress up.' I sat up sluggishly. Kavya eyed me. 'You need to eat something, Jhanvi; I'll order room service. You get our outfits together okay?'

I nodded and began unpacking our bags. I wasn't hungry, but I knew that fighting her would be pointless and not worth it so soon after our last fight. I selected a black lace mini dress for Kavya, and a tan suede leather jacket that I would tie around her waist. The look would be finished with a black bowler hat that I would match with my own. For myself, I chose a loose-fitting mini dress; it was black, and mandala patterns in pinks, yellows and greens broke the solid colour. Black boots for both of us, I thought.

Kavya opened the door for room service. She had ordered samosas and sandwiches. My stomach told me that my previous thought that I was not hungry was incorrect. Together, we sat and ate, drinking our iced tea and speaking excitedly about the line-up. By the time we were dressed, I had taken over fifteen photos for later posts.

Entering the festival took my breath away. The massive stage was overshadowed only by the biggest Ferris wheel I had ever seen. Our VIP bands saw us being ushered quickly to a tent decorated with Burn Promotions paraphernalia, food and alcohol on tap. Kavya squealed, making her way to the gift table. A hand touched my lower back; I swung around and was met by Gaurav, smiling smugly.

'Don't touch me, Gaurav; you lost that privilege a long time ago.'

He took a step back, pretending my words had wounded him. 'Look Jhanvi, we have two days here together. I just came over to say that I think we are both mature enough to get through this without any more drama.'

I rolled my eyes at him. 'Fine,' I said. 'Where's your hanger-on?'

'She's in the hotel room.' He brushed a hand through his hair. 'She's angry; she says she can see I still have feelings for you.'

'That's ridiculous,' I shot back. 'You should try dating in your age group, though. Children do tend to have tantrums.'

He shook his head at me. 'Always a smart answer. I do miss that.' He took a step forward.

My heart dropped to my stomach. I put my hands up to stop him from moving any closer. 'No, Gaurav,' I said. 'You hurt me, we're over, and I am not going to be the reason that girl is devastated. I know all too well what it feels like to be cheated on. Or have you forgotten?'

I turned my back on him, eyeing the space for Kavya. She was talking to a guy near the gift table; she seemed to be enjoying herself. A woman walked past me with drinks on a tray. I grabbed two, downing the first without thinking. The cold sour liquor sent shivers down my back; the second drink seemed not to have any effect. I placed the glasses back on the tray. Kavya looked over to me and smiled. I smiled back, motioning that I was going to look around; I made my way to the bar.

'Vodka,' I said, 'straight.' Looking over my shoulder, I saw that Gaurav was still standing where I'd left him; his eyes were fixed on me. I turned to the bartender. 'Make it a double.'

10

ASHRAY

Isn't friendship strange? The notion that two or more people can find each other in the maddening crowd and exist together, to make each other happy, to offer comfort and support in ways that our blood relations never could. That a love could be forged between two people, a love that exists not to perpetuate the population of humankind, but rather to allow us to bond with another person who completes some part of us that we have lost along the way.

'Hey, hey,' Rishi said with a broad smile as I approached the platform. 'Looking smart!'

I smiled back, offering my hand.

'You ready to relax and have a party?' he asked as we stepped onto the train that would take us to the airport. I nodded, self-conscious about my old travel case and sneakers. I felt terrible that this friend I had made less than a week ago was paying for me to go away with him. Maa, of course, told me that some people want to give, that was what made them happiest, but I was already formulating plans on how to pay him back. I knew he would not accept money. I would need to find some creative way to repay him. On the train ride, Rishi chatted about how BusinessForward had changed his life. I listened intently, but subconsciously I scanned the carriage. He dug his elbow in my side and grinned.

'You looking for that girl, Ashray? I don't think she will be on this train,' he said with a laugh. I blushed; I hadn't realised that I was looking around that obviously.

'You should have just asked her for her number; it would be a lot easier than searching for her on the train every day.'

He let out a laugh, and I joined him, realising how ridiculous I was being.

At the airport, Rishi pulled out his credit card to pay for the flights. I removed the roll of money Maa had given me before I left, in an attempt to pay. He dismissed me, taking the roll and shoving it deep into my pocket. He leaned over and whispered, 'You can't wave money around like that if you don't want it pickpocketed.'

I looked around frantically for potential thieves. He laughed. 'Look, Ashray, this time it's my turn, next time it's yours, okay? By next year's festival you will be earning more than me anyway.' He patted me on the back.

I didn't understand why he had so much faith in me, but I smiled and nodded, hoping that what he said was the truth. We passed through to the departure hall. Passengers lay sleeping on the metal airport chairs, some with their bags under their heads, others with them tucked tightly under their seats. We sat down, and I pushed my frayed duffle bag under my seat, hoping no one would notice it.

'So, where did you get that roll of money?' Rishi asked. I shifted uncomfortably in my seat; there was no point lying to him.

'I give Maa some of my salary every month. It's meant for her to spend on herself, but she always puts it away in a tin and spends it on me on my birthday.'

'I guess it's the nature of every Indian mother,' he said with a smile.

'Maybe,' I said.

We spoke for forty minutes while we waited to board our flight. Rishi had recently been dumped by his girlfriend, and was eager to get away to take his mind off the ugliness of their breakup. He had truly thought he would marry this girl, but it turned out that she had no intention of marrying him; she had stayed for the money and left him for a wealthy doctor in Kolkata. He was wounded but was not swearing off finding someone to spend his life with.

Unlike me, he'd had an easy childhood. He came from a large family. His parents weren't wealthy, but they did not struggle. His father had spent his whole life working for an international company, which rewarded him well in his retirement. It seemed a natural progression for Rishi to work for a company like BusinessForward. When he landed the job at BusinessForward, his parents packed up their lives in Mumbai and moved halfway across the world to live out their retirement on the beaches of Mexico. They were close to the US for healthcare, and his dad's retirement fund meant they lived a very comfortable life away from the hustle and bustle of Mumbai.

Walking up the steps to the plane, I froze.

He tugged on my arm. 'What's the matter, Ashray? You've never flown before?' I shook my head. Wide-eyed, he locked his arm into mine. 'Well, this will be a great first then, my friend,' he reassured me. 'Next year, you pay for business class.'

I laughed; he had a way of making me feel comfortable. We walked into the plane and looked for our seats. The flight was full of festival-goers taking advantage of the cheap late-night flight. I put my bag on the ground in front of the seat. Rishi tapped me on the back, motioning for me to put it in the overhead compartment. Embarrassed, I did so.

'Here, sit by the window,' he said. I squeezed my way over. He showed me how to put my seatbelt on and went into a long-winded discussion about how it would feel as the plane took off, banked and evened out. Announcements came on, but he continued to talk, and I listened intently. Finally, he stopped and, grinning widely, knocked my elbow with his.

'Hey Ashray, look out the window.' I turned; around us, the night sky was mottled with the city smog. Below, the lights of

Mumbai burned like torches in the distance. I gasped. We had taken off during Rishi's speech, and I hadn't even noticed. He laughed at the expression on my face; doubled over, I joined him. The landing wasn't quite as smooth. I anticipated every bump, convinced the plane's wing would fall off, plunging us all into a fiery death. Rishi laughed at me, but offered as much reassurance as he could.

We retrieved our bags and made our way through the airport. At the taxi rank, Rishi haggled with a driver for a good fare. He told me we would camp outside the main stage grounds where all the other revellers took short rests. He seemed apologetic, but I was grateful, regardless. By the time we made it to the campsite, the sun was about to rise. Multicoloured tents littered the horizon; people were making coffee on fires, some looked a little worse for wear from the previous night's party.

We set up the tent together, although Rishi seemed a little lost on what to do; finally, something I could contribute on. He laid out two sleeping bags and two pillows and insisted we get some sleep before going to the festival. I protested at first, excited to see what was going on, but I had to admit that I was exhausted. My head had barely touched the pillow before darkness enveloped me. I slept soundly; no dreams came. I woke up with Rishi waving a hot cup of black coffee next to me. I sat up, grateful for the sweet hot liquid. I felt it was the only thing that would revive me from my deep slumber.

'We'll get something to eat and then go and check it out, okay?' he said, sipping on his coffee. I could hear the music filtering through the grounds, the sound of people screaming in appreciation of their music heroes.

'Sounds like fun,' I said.

My stomach grumbled and Rishi burst out laughing. 'Sounds like you need to eat. Here,' he handed me a bottle of water. 'There are no showers here; you will need to use this to wash your face. Then put your shoes on, and we can find something to eat.'

I took the bottle outside the tent and, carefully pouring water into my scooped hand, I washed off the remaining sleep. I patted my wet hand on the back of my neck. Re-entering the tent, I handed Rishi the bottle and grabbed my sneakers.

'Where's that money,' Rishi asked. I tapped my pocket to indicate it was with me. 'Good,' he said. 'Come, let's find something to eat.

Together, we browsed the food stalls; I had never seen such a variety of foods—there was something from every culture. Rishi insisted we have Mexican Molletes; he said he lived on them when he went to visit his parents a year ago. To me, they looked like regular sandwiches, but once I bit into one, I understood why he wanted them so badly. With our food, he bought two cans of soda. We looked for an empty spot to sit and eat our lunch without being bumped around. The red clay was hot from being baked in the sun; it left dark red smudges on my jeans and sneakers. I bent to dust them off before realising it was futile while we still sat eating.

'And all these women in their best outfits,' he said, eyeing me trying to dust my jeans. 'Seems pointless, don't you think?' I nodded, chewing on my torta. 'It's nice to look at though,' he said, laughing, and I almost choked at his brazenness. 'No, seriously, Ashray, look at this one coming from behind you. She is wearing a full-length skirt and a crop top. Very nice,' he said. I couldn't bring myself to turn around and look; I didn't know how to do it without making it seem obvious. 'Don't worry, she'll walk past us soon, but I wish you could see her face. She is quite pretty.' I sat dead still, hoping the woman couldn't hear Rishi openly gushing about her. As she walked past, Rishi stood up. My mouth dropped open; how did this man have so much confidence?

'Hi, I'm Rishi,' he said and held out his hand. The woman stopped; I kept my head down, sure she was getting ready to tell him off. 'This is my friend, Ashray. We've come to the music festival as a last-minute getaway. What about you?' I took a bite of my torta, waiting for the backlash.

'We've also come for a getaway,' she replied, shaking Rishi's hand. She turned to me, hand outstretched.

'Sakshi,' I mumbled, mouth full of food. She let out a giggle; I must have looked a real sight. Rishi could not contain his excitement.

'This is the girl from the train?' he shouted. I blushed.

'Yes,' she said, smiling warmly, never taking her eyes off of mine. 'I'm the girl from the train.'

II
JHANVI

The clear liquid warmed me from the inside. I ordered another, poured it into my empty water bottle, and walked over to Kavya. She was happily chatting to a group of influencers who were telling her how this festival was way better than last year's. Tonight, they would launch a massive hot air balloon that would project lasers into the crowd. I looked at my friend; she seemed so happy and content. She handed me a gin cooler.

'I didn't say you couldn't drink at all,' she said, eyeing my bottle of water.

'Thanks,' I responded, feeling guilty for deceiving her. I sipped on the cooler, asking questions from the group about how they got into social media and how they grew their following. The vodka and two shots from earlier gave me more confidence than usual.

A tall man wearing a pair of jeans and a harassed look on his face walked into the marquee.

'The A-listers will begin playing shortly,' he shouted. 'If you would all like to make your way to the VIP area within the next hour, that would be great.'

I turned to Kavya and told her I wanted to look around, and that I would meet her at the VIP area in thirty minutes. She protested, but I insisted that she stay and chat with her new friends. At the bar, I ordered another double vodka neat and poured it into my water bottle before exiting the tent. Outside, partygoers were dancing to the sounds of electronic music; the sky filled with smoke from the stage. A single DJ stood on the vast wood and metal platform, one arm in the air, the other pressing buttons furiously. I walked towards the Ferris wheel and placed my phone on my selfie stick. Posing, I took a few photos. I wanted a full body shot as well; I needed to give the impression that I had at least a crew of one to assist me with my styling and photography. Two men and a young woman in a skirt and crop top ambled past.

'Excuse me,' I touched the woman's arm. 'I love your skirt.' She smiled warmly back at me, not offering the usual explanation of where she had bought it. 'Would you mind taking a photo of me?'

'No problem at all,' she said. I handed her my phone, showing her how to set it to professional before taking the picture. I stood in front of the imposing Ferris wheel and smiled. For the second photo, I acted as if I was laughing, and for the third, I placed my hand on my hat and leaped into the air.

'Thank you,' I said as I took my phone back. She nodded and carried on walking with the men as if nothing had happened. I swiped through the photos, impressed with how they had come out. I locked my phone, put it in my small waist bag, and walked towards the VIP area. Gaurav was already there, his arm draped over a groupie, smiling for a photo. My stomach turned. I opened my water bottle and downed the contents. My body shivered. I walked into the VIP area confidently. Thankfully, Kavya joined shortly after, with the other influencers in tow. She handed me a cooler.

'You all right?' she asked, eying me.

'Fine,' I replied, faking the biggest smile I could. 'Look at these.' I eagerly showed her the pictures that the woman had taken of me a few minutes ago.

'Those are amazing, Jhanvi!' she shouted over the announcement; speakers boomed as the first A-lister hit the stage.

The set lasted an hour. My head was spinning, I needed to find somewhere I could freshen up or get water to drink. I leaned into Kavya and shouted in her ear that I was going to look for a bathroom. She nodded and made as if she was going to follow, but I put my hand out, stopping her. I walked back to the VIP marquee tent. Flashing my armband at the bouncer, I was let in. I walked up to the bar to order water, but before I could speak, a voice called me from the back of the tent. I didn't need to turn to see who it was.

'Make it a double vodka,' I said. I would need it if I was going to have to deal with Gaurav's girlfriend. Turning around, I saw her gesturing wildly for me to come over. She was draped across a leather couch, a group of men around her, all anxiously vying for her attention. I took a deep breath and walked over to her.

'Jhanvi!' she shrieked. 'Come. Sit!' Reluctantly I sat next to her. 'Meet my friends,' she waved her hands around before leaning in close to me. 'I don't know their names,' she said and giggled. I smiled back, weakly. 'Listen,' she said, clearly intoxicated. 'I just need to apologise for what went on in the plane yesterday,' she said sincerely. 'I am not as stupid and naive as people think I am, Jhanvi. I know he is not faithful; but I'm not ready to give up all of this just yet.' Thinking back to how I played down Gaurav's indiscretions, I felt sorry for her. 'Anyway. My name is Latika,' she said.

A waiter came up and placed a tray of shots on the round table in front of us. Latika grinned.

'Well, Latika, if we are now friends, then I guess it's time to start a party then.' I grinned back and handed her a shot. We clinked our glasses and downed the syrupy liquid. I told the waiter to keep them coming and dug into my bag to pull out my phone.

'Selfie,' I yelled, as half-naked men and Latika leapt into the frame. Reaching forward, I grabbed another glass and downed its contents. I stood up and swayed, but recovered by pretending to dance. Latika laughed and joined me. The music was loud, hypnotic even, and I allowed the alcohol to numb the pain I felt inside. Latika took copious amounts of pictures; I only hoped that she would not post them online without first passing them by me. As the night progressed, people joined us, some for the photo opportunity, and others for a quick drink. Gaurav came in and tried to start an argument with Latika, but I quickly intervened, telling him to get lost. Then Kavya walked into the tent. I could see the anger etched on her face. I smiled, trying to defuse the argument that was coming.

'Have you been here the whole time?' she yelled at me.

'Oh, relax, Kavya. Look! We have a new friend!' I draped my arm around Latika, whose swaying caught me off-guard. I stumbled. Kavya grabbed my arm and dragged me from the marquee. Outside, I snatched my arm back.

'What are you doing?' I shouted at her. I could see the anger rise as she compressed her lips. 'I'm having fun, and all you have done since we left my apartment is police me. I'm sick of it, Kavya! You're not my mother, and you're not my keeper! You wouldn't even be here if it wasn't for me!' I could see that the last sentence hurt her. 'Look,' I said, 'I'm just having a little fun. This whole thing with Puneet, and now Gaurav being here, it's just a little too much.' I reached out to touch her arm. She recoiled from me.

'That's fine, Jhanvi. You don't have to worry about me policing you anymore. I'm done.' She walked away, disappearing into the crowd. I lifted my hand to my face; this was why I never expressed how I felt. It always ended in unnecessary conflict. I turned around and walked back into the marquee where Latika was waiting for me, drink in hand.

'Your friend is not coming back?' she slurred as she handed me the drink. I shook my head, not wanting to tell her about our argument. 'Oh well. More for us.' She knocked her shot glass against mine, spilling half its contents before downing the rest. I followed suit, swallowing quickly. My stomach was beginning to feel strange.

From behind me, one of the men that had been with Latika when I first arrived shouted, 'Party foul! That's another shot.' He handed each of us another glass. This time the liquid was red and smelled of cinnamon. I shook my head; the room was spinning.

'Oh, come on, Jhanvi. Don't be a spoilsport now,' Latika said. I took the glass and downed it. My stomach instantly objected. I walked away as best I could. I needed some air. Outside, the night was muggy; it did nothing for the nausea I felt. I stumbled forward through the crowds, trying to make my way to the portable toilets set up for festival-goers. Leaning against one, I tried the door. Occupied. I moved on to the next and the next and the next. I cursed. I couldn't be sick. Not so close to the VIP area, and definitely nowhere that anyone could document it. In the distance, in the grounds that housed all the campers, a few cubicles stood with their doors open. I made my way back through the crowds, bumping into people. My vision was blurry, my feet unstable. Walking between the tents was proving to be a little more challenging than I had expected. I tripped over a rope and fell on my hands and knees. Looking up, I saw the cubicles. I began to crawl slowly. From behind me, two men laughed.

'You all right there?' The man's voice sounded strange, distant. I opened my mouth to reply. Darkness closed in on me.

It was quiet, other than the sound of a few footsteps. The sun was filling my room. I rolled over, not opening my eyes. Something wet touched my cheek and I sat straight up. My head pounded and my mouth felt like I hadn't had water in weeks. I looked around. 'Where the hell am I?' I didn't recognise my voice. This wasn't my hotel room. Bright green awnings surrounded me. I was sitting in a sleeping bag. My clothes, full of vomit, were strewn next to me. I wiped my face and instantly gagged. Cold, sticky sick clung to my face. I grabbed a polystyrene cup and emptied what was left in my stomach. I couldn't think. My head was too sore. Realising I was only in my underwear, I grabbed the sleeping bag and pulled it to my chest, half expecting that whoever put me there would return. I looked around hurriedly for my bag. It was under my soiled dress. Opening it, I discovered my cash taken, but my phone was still there.

I tapped the screen, praying that there was still enough battery power to message Kavya. The screen came to life, and notifications streamed in. What had I posted? I opened my contact list and typed in K. Kavya's number popped up; I hesitated for a moment before pressing the dial button.

She answered immediately. 'Jhanvi,' she said. I sighed in relief before tears began to fall. 'Jhanvi. What's wrong?'

'I'm in a tent. I don't know where. And there is vomit on my clothes,' I sobbed. 'Kavya. I am naked, and I don't know what happened.'

She cursed. 'Listen to me. Put your dress on and stand outside the tent. Jhanvi? Jhanvi are you listening to me?'

I sobbed into my phone. 'Yes,' I said finally.

'It's early. Nobody will see you, okay? I will bring another dress you can put on for the walk back.' She hung up the phone. I slid out of the sleeping bag and grabbed my dress, trying to rub off the putrid stench of last night's sick. I crawled out of the tent. From behind me, a man shouted something about me always being on my hands and knees. My stomach lurched, and tears fell freely. I stood up. In the distance, I could see Kavya looking around frantically. I lifted my arm and waved. She came running.

'Get back in there and put this on,' she said. I obeyed. She poked her head into the tent. 'Give me that dress; we will need it if the police want evidence.'

'Police?' I said, my head throbbing. 'No, Kavya, please. I just want to get back to the room and have a shower. Please.'

She saw how upset I was and nodded. 'Come, where are your shoes?'

I shrugged; I had no idea where they were. A fresh wave of tears began. Kavya put her arm around me. 'Leave them; they weren't that great anyway. You have your bag?' I nodded, wiping away my tears. She walked me across the camping grounds to our hotel room. Switching on the shower, she helped me undress before turning and closing the bathroom door. Crouching down into a ball, I let the water run over me, washing last night off, trying to remember what happened. I began to sob again.

12
ASHRAY

'Look at this stage,' Sakshi gushed. 'And we have to go on the Ferris wheel!' Her enthusiasm was contagious. I agreed, although the sheer size of it frightened me. Rishi and Sakshi were chatting nonstop; I didn't mind. I needed time to process what was going on around me. I had never attended anything quite as extravagant as this before. Music was playing from the biggest speakers I had ever seen, while people hung around waiting excitedly for some of the acts to take the stage. Everywhere I looked, people were on their phones. A woman stood in front of us taking photos with a selfie stick, the big wheel behind her. She stopped Sakshi, complimenting her on her outfit, and although I sensed Sakshi didn't want to stop and talk to the woman, she obliged, even helping her take a series of ridiculous photos.

Rishi turned his back to what was happening and raised his eyebrows. I whispered to him that a girl like that was way out of both our leagues. I thought for a moment that he might take what I said as a challenge; instead, he shrugged and began talking about which DJs would be playing tonight. Once the girls were done taking their photos, we walked towards the big wheel. Sakshi slid her arm into mine; my heart began to race. Rishi knocked me with his elbow and winked; I felt the heat rising to my cheeks. I knocked him back and, turning to Sakshi, realised she had seen the entire exchange. I coughed. 'What do you say we go on that big wheel then?' I said to her, trying to divert her attention from what had happened.

'Yes please!' she said and tugged on my arm, directing me towards the line of people waiting for the ride.

'I'll go and get us tickets then,' Rishi said. He smiled and winked at me. I mock scowled back at him before turning my attention back to Sakshi.

'So, Sakshi, we never really got to talking properly about what you do on Monday.'

She giggled at my attempt to be sophisticated. 'Well, Ashray,' she answered in a tone that matched mine, 'I'm studying to be a nurse. Not full time, my mum needs me because of her health issues, but I'm hoping to be done by the end of the year.'

I smiled. Clever, beautiful and kind, I thought.

'What did the doctor say about your mum? I mean, if you don't mind me asking.' I blushed.

'She has this really rare condition where her heart is on the other side of her body. It's really a miracle I was even born, and she survived,' she explained. I listened as Sakshi spoke about her Maa and medicine, taking in her voice and her face while she talked. I couldn't help but feel like I was falling for this woman. I didn't know much about love; I had thought that I loved my high school girlfriend, but she dumped me when we went to college. My Maa told me that your first love is very rarely your only love, and rarely your great love. Rishi joined us as Sakshi finished her story. He shoved two tickets in my hand.

'There's only two here.' I looked at him.

'I know,' he winked. I excused myself from Sakshi and grabbed Rishi's arm.

'We didn't come here this weekend for you to be my wingman,' I protested. Rishi burst out laughing and patted my back.

'Ashray. You spent five days travelling to work in the same train carriage, all to find the girl you spoke to on day one, and now here she is. Amongst all these thousands of people, *she* happened to walk past us. That's serendipity. The universe is speaking to you both, and who am I to stand in the way of the universe?'

'But what will you do?' I asked.

'I'm going to stay down here and watch that you two love birds don't get up to anything I wouldn't do.' He laughed and smacked my back again.

'Ashray!' Sakshi called from the line. People were getting off the wheel and those waiting began to move to the front.

'Go,' Rishi insisted. I took a deep breath and joined Sakshi in the queue. Instantly she locked arms with me again. Butterflies exploded in my stomach.

'Everything all right?' she asked. I nodded. Everything was perfect.

The ride was exhilarating. Sakshi clutched my arm as the wheel turned, and we both laughed with the rush of its drops and lifts. As the ride came to an end, she leaned over and kissed me on the cheek. I took her hand in mine as we got off the big wheel. Rishi was talking to a young woman who was animatedly explaining something to him.

Sakshi looked at me and said, 'I wonder what's going on there.'

We walked hand in hand to where Rishi was standing. A new feeling of butterflies erupted in my stomach, and my mind yearned to know this woman deeper. I could see my life with her, though I barely knew her.

'Ashray! How was the ride?' He looked down to see me holding hands with Sakshi and gave me a thumbs up. I shook my head.

'This is my friend Latika,' he said, indicating the woman with him. 'Latika's boyfriend is some big shot social media star who has a VIP pass.'

'He's an idiot! Right now he's running around trying to get back together with his ex-girlfriend while he is still dating me!' she yelled.

'Anyway,' Rishi said with a laugh, 'we're going to wait until

the VIPs leave their special waiting area, and then Latika is
going to get us into a private party. What do you say?'

Sakshi answered, 'Actually, Rishi, I was hoping that Ashray
and I could spend a little time together tonight. I have to fly
back tomorrow, so ...' she trailed off.

'You just give him your number this time,' Rishi said,
before turning his attention back to the young woman who
immediately began complaining about her boyfriend again.
I thought I saw the hurt in his eyes, but before I could say
anything, he was walking off with Latika.

'So,' Sakshi turned to me, 'what should we do?'

We eventually decided to sit right at the back of the stage area,
where we would be able to talk without straining too much.
I touched my jeans pocket to make sure my money was still
there. I led Sakshi back to the stall where Rishi and I had
bought the Mexican sandwiches; I bought us each one along
with a soda. We ambled back to the stage area, eating and
laughing about stories from our childhood.

She told me that she grew up in an average middle-class
home. Her father was a doctor, and her mother, a nurse. After
her father retired from his job and her mother began showing
symptoms of her health problem, Sakshi had quit full-time
nursing school so that she could attend to her.

I told Sakshi that I was an orphan, about how I was left on
the doorsteps of the orphanage, and how I never knew who my
parents were but that my Maa was for all intents and purposes
my mother. She raised me, sacrificed so much for me. When I
told her that I would like to own a home where Maa would be
able to live with my wife and me, Sakshi gushed. She loved the
idea. I was relieved, I couldn't even think of falling in love with
a woman who did not share the same vision for our future.

I felt comfortable with this woman I hardly knew, and
she, I hoped, felt comfortable with me. The evening was spent

catching up on all of the things we had not yet spoken about; the conversation flowed freely. She only let go of my hand when she had to. Around midnight, she laid her head on my chest; I felt her yawn. Any thoughts I had of not falling in love with her were long gone; a battle that couldn't be won. My heart had overruled my head the moment her head found its spot over my heart.

'Are you tired?' I asked, concerned that she had an early flight back to Mumbai.

'I am, but I want to finish this set, all right?' I couldn't see her smile, but I imagined her warm smile reaching her eyes. Silently, we sat and listened to the music, watching the laser show. It was the most incredible thing I had ever seen. When the set was done, I helped Sakshi up and walked her through the camping grounds to her tent.

'Heard from Rishi?' she asked. I shook my head and was about to say something when Sakshi stopped dead and pointed in front of us. A woman was crawling through the tents; she looked ill and had definitely had too much to drink.

'You all right there?' I shouted. She collapsed, and Sakshi ran to her side. I followed, not quite as quickly, afraid of what I was going to see.

'Quickly Ashray, she is sick. I need to roll her onto her side.' I kneeled and helped Sakshi roll the limp girl over. The smell of alcohol and vomit was overpowering.

'What do we do?' I asked. I didn't have a clue what the protocol was for a drunk girl lying in a camping ground.

'We can't leave her here,' Sakshi answered. 'Do you think Rishi will be back tonight?' I shook my head. I highly doubted Rishi would find his way back to our tent before the sun rose.

'Here, help me get her into my tent.' I picked the girl up and did my best to get her into Sakshi's bright green, domed tent without dropping her.

Sakshi asked me to leave the room while she undressed the woman and turned her on her side. I rummaged through her bag, trying to find some identification. Her phone was on, but it was password-protected, and I had no chance of guessing the code. The only other thing in her bag was some cash. Remembering what Rishi had told me about pickpockets, I rolled her money up and stuck it deep inside her boots, which I then placed at the entrance of the tent behind Sakshi's towels. When Sakshi was satisfied that the woman wouldn't choke if she got sick again, we walked hand in hand back to Rishi's and my tent. Sakshi would sleep on my side of the tent tonight, and I would take Rishi's spot.

'In the orphanage, I was bullied pretty badly. Always the sullen child who thought too deeply and felt too strongly,' I said as we settled in our sleeping bags.

'Really?' she said, propping herself up on her elbow.

'I don't know why. To this day, I feel deeply about things I am passionate about, you know? My career and aspirations, my Maa and now …' I trailed off, scared that she would reject me, terrified of what it would mean if she saw me as something less than what I saw her.

'And now, Ashray?'

I took the leap, remembering that, if I didn't tell her, she would never know. 'And now you.' The tent seemed to fill with tension, a thick silence that, for me, seemed never-ending.

'I feel deeply for you as well, Ashray. I can't describe it.' She paused for a moment, holding her breath seemingly at the same time as I held mine. 'The moment I saw you on the train, I had this feeling that I needed to know you. That you may change my life. I was so angry with myself for not getting your number. But fate intervened, didn't it?' I couldn't see her face in the darkness, but I felt the warmth of her smile.

We lay there for almost two hours, speaking of our childhood and how we had changed as the responsibilities of being an adult took over. In that short period of time, hunkered down in a canvas dome, in a place I didn't know, I gave my heart to her and she gave hers to me. It was too early to say the words we felt, ridiculous to even contemplate uttering them into the darkness, but for me the emotions were overwhelmingly real. I wanted to crawl across the short section of ground that separated us. I wanted to hold her tightly in my arms and drift off into a dream where we could live in bliss, but it was too soon.

Before we rolled over to sleep, I looked across to her.

'You're one special person; you know that?'

'You're not too bad yourself,' she said. 'Goodnight, Ashray. See you in the morning.'

I went to sleep with a smile on my face. A new job that was amazing and, quite possibly, a new girlfriend. 'Yes, Ashray,' I thought to myself. 'Life is very definitely changing.'

13

JHANVI

'They will be expecting you this morning, Jhanvi,' Kavya said as she handed me a glass of orange juice and two tablets for my pounding head.

I knew she was right, but I did not want to see Gaurav this morning, and I did not want to rehash last night with Latika. I nodded, not wanting to have another argument; I didn't have the strength for another emotional conflict.

'Come, lay down for a bit, I will order breakfast,' she said, and patted the bed. I obeyed, resting my head on a pillow as I watched her order food. I waited for the interrogation. Sure enough, when Kavya put down the phone, she asked, 'What is the last thing you remember from last night?' I groaned. I didn't want to recall anything, didn't need that stark reminder of how I had lost control.

'Gaurav just got to me,' I began. 'I went back to the tent and Latika …' I trailed off. 'It just got out of hand. It won't happen again.' I said. I could see that she wanted to push me further but there was a knock on the door just then. Kavya thanked the server and closed the door behind him. She brought the tray of food to the bed. The mixture of aromas made my stomach turn, and I quickly closed the silver lid back over the plate. Kavya handed me a slice of bread. 'You must eat something Jhanvi,' she said, concern in her eyes. I obliged to avoid another argument. We sat in silence as we ate breakfast, Kavya eagerly adding more and more to the originally agreed upon bread. By the time I had finished eating, my head felt slightly better.

'Did you at least get enough photos of last night to post to your account?' she asked.

I dove across the bed for my phone, which was on charge. Putting in the pin to unlock it, I opened the gallery. I sighed; there were some decent photos. Quickly, I picked two from earlier in the evening and carefully edited them to ensure nobody could guess how much I'd actually had to drink. I made sure to add the hashtags agreed upon with Burn Promotions. Immediately the PR manager responded. I cursed. They were watching my account, and I was late in posting. Quickly, I added a few more photos to my story, making sure to gush about how much I appreciated being allowed to work with the company. Hearts filled my screen, and my follower count grew quickly. I smiled, thinking that I had adequately saved something that could easily have turned bad.

'Everything okay?' Kavya interrupted my thoughts.

'All fine,' I said, locking my phone. 'What are we going to wear today? We'll need to make a good lasting impression on our final day.' Kavya eyed me again, and then probably figuring out that she wasn't going to get anything else out of me about the previous night, she opened her travel case.

'I was thinking of this red dress,' she said, holding up the loose-fitting cotton red and white dress I'd packed in for her earlier in the week. I nodded in approval, and asked her to bring my case over. Opening it, I found a white cotton long-sleeve button-up shirt and handed it to her. 'You can wear this with it; leave it unbuttoned though, and I'll help you roll the sleeves.' For myself, I pulled out a pair of white high-waisted shorts with grey elephants printed on them, and an oversized grey shirt that I had modified into a front-tying crop top. I chose a pair of large gold-framed sunglasses to go with the outfit.

Kavya headed to the bathroom to get ready and a message pinged through on my phone. I unlocked it.

'*Hi bestie, you disappeared last night. Feeling all right? L.*'

I groaned out loud and typed a quick, polite response before locking my phone and throwing it on the bed.

'Everything all right?' Kavya was standing at the bathroom door, toothbrush in hand.

'Fine. Gaurav's new girlfriend thinks we are BFFs all of a sudden,' I said and smiled, trying to downplay my annoyance with myself.

'Well, that position is taken,' Kavya said, rolling her eyes. Another message came through. I ignored it to get up and get dressed. Together, we walked out into the warm air; the smell of the ocean was a pleasant change from the usual Mumbai city smells. My stomach, still unhappy with me, protested loudly. We chatted as we walked to the VIP area, discussing Latika and Gaurav and how their relationship was doomed to fail regardless of whether I was on this trip or not. Inside the tent, a waiter pushed forward a tray of champagne glasses filled with orange juice.

'Champagne and orange juice for the ladies?'

I could feel Kavya's eyes on me. I shook my head. 'Just plain orange juice,' I said.

'You will have to go to the bar for that,' the waiter said and winked, probably insinuating that he understood I had a hangover.

In a corner, Gaurav was speaking with some Burn Promotions PR people, while Latika sat not far from him, arms crossed and clearly sulking. Kavya leaned in and said, 'Your bestie is over there, waiting for you.' I shot her a look, and she burst out laughing.

The group of influencers she was with last night were sitting on one of the leather couches, drinking coffee; they smiled and waved for her to come over.

'Go,' I told her, 'I'm just going to get myself an orange juice and I will be right over.'

'You sure?'

I nodded before walking towards the bar. Thankfully, new bar staff were serving drinks this morning. I ordered the largest orange juice they had and took a big sip. The ice-cold sour liquid was like being splashed with cold water, and I felt instantly more awake.

'Rough night?' I turned to see a tall man in a pair of white linen shorts and a white Burn Promotions shirt.

He extended his hand and said, 'I'm Arnav.' I smiled weakly, and he burst out laughing. 'I'm the PR manager assigned to you for the festival. I sent you the original message.' As I shook his hand, I wondered if I was going to be berated for my lack of posts last night.

'Are you enjoying yourself?'

I nodded, unsure of what to say.

'I'm not going to keep you long. I just came over to say that, although we understand your feed is more curated,' he emphasised the word curated and I felt myself blush, 'we would like a little more live content today. Okay?' I couldn't find the words to make an excuse for why I hadn't posted last night. Again, I nodded and internally screamed at myself for not finding my voice. 'We aren't unhappy with you, Jhanvi; it's just that these things tend to benefit both the promoter and the promotee, when they are posted at the moment.'

'I understand completely,' I said, finally finding the words. 'I will make the relevant adjustments for today's posts.' Arnav smiled and wished me luck for the remainder of the day. As he walked away, I put my elbows on the bar counter to steady myself. My heart was racing and I felt as if I was going to be sick again.

'You all right?' The phrase made my heart leap. Somewhere in the recesses of my mind, I remembered it from last night.

'Could I have a double vodka?' I said, sliding the glass with orange juice across the bar counter. The barman smiled knowingly. I needed to calm my nerves, and I knew one drink wouldn't make that much of a difference. Picking up my glass, I walked towards Kavya. A hand grabbed my arm, swinging me around.

It was Gaurav. 'You need to stay out of my life, Jhanvi,' he said, squeezing my arm. 'I don't know what you told Latika last night, but I came back to my room to be greeted with her acting like a drunken slut with some loser marketing nerd.' I pulled my arm back, spilling orange juice on his white sneakers. 'Just perfect,' he spat at me. 'I don't need my reputation pulled through the mud because of a bitter ex and a stupid woman!'

'As opposed to your stellar reputation when you recorded yourself naked and allowed it to leak onto social media?' I shot back.

'Get lost, asshole!' Kavya said, appearing from behind me, hands on her hips, ready to take on Gaurav. He put his hands up in defeat. Not wanting to cause a scene, he walked away to sit with Latika in the corner. Kavya rolled her eyes and locked her arm in mine. We spent the remainder of the day watching musicians and taking photos; I made sure to post photos as requested by Arnav. Every second trip to the bar was mine, and by the fourth trip, I was beginning to feel a bit buzzed. I knew we had to fly back tomorrow morning; I couldn't afford to have a repeat of last night. Eventually, I convinced Kavya that I needed to go back to the room, tasking her with taking photos of the night set for me to post.

Back in the room, I opened the minibar and tiny bottles of alcohol stared back at me. I was tired, really tired. I picked up the hotel room phone and ordered three energy drinks. Once they arrived, I poured a small bottle of vodka into my drink, flopped down on the bed and opened my phone.

I opened my latest post: 123,482 likes. I stared, mouth open. I pulled the screen down to refresh. 'This must be a mistake,' I thought. The screen reloaded—125,801 likes. I quickly tapped on my follower account: +15,000 followers in the last eight hours. I put my phone down on the bed in disbelief. It started as a smile, but quickly maniacal laughter overtook me. I composed myself, belly aching, I downed my drink before opening another and taking a sip to make enough room for the bottle of vodka. I opened my phone and stared at the numbers again.

Opening my messages and selecting Kavya, I typed a quick message.

'Changed my mind. Coming back.'

I rummaged through my suitcase to find something appropriate for the night set. I put on a black, short-sleeved bodysuit and a pair of loose-fitting cobalt blue, high-waisted pants. I slipped on a pair of gold sandals and a gold headband I was saving for the final night. I downed what was left of my second drink before emptying the contents of the third can and third mini vodka into a bottle supplied by Burn Promotions. I took the empty cans and bottles and put them in the bin in the bathroom, being careful to hide them underneath the garbage already in there. I grabbed my phone and bag and walked outside. I wasn't too sure if it was the energy drinks or the follower count, but I was on a high, and I was hooked, needing another perfect photo to bring in the likes. I flashed my wristband at the entrance to the VIP area; loud music and lasers thumped through me, matching my heartbeat. I walked up to Kavya, giving her a hug as she handed me a gin cooler, the same type we had the night before. I waved my hand, not wanting to repeat the same mistakes as last night; I gestured towards my bottle. She didn't need to know what was in it.

When we landed in Mumbai on Monday morning, I was changed. I had almost fifty thousand new followers, an inbox filled with businesses who wanted to work with me, and a new way to keep my energy levels up. No thoughts of Puneet entered my mind, no reminders of failure. Only the high. I was hooked, and I didn't care.

14
ASHRAY

I was hoping to catch up on some sleep, but Rishi had other ideas. In the taxi to the airport, he spoke nonstop about his time in the VIP tent and how he was partying with some influencer girls. He was hoping that he would be able to get the one woman's number after he walked her to her hotel room, but her boyfriend barged in just as he was pouring the woman a drink from the hotel minibar. Her boyfriend had let him leave without the mandatory beating he believed Rishi deserved.

Drunk, and with no bearings as to where our tent was, he went back to the main stage, eventually falling asleep at the back of the grounds. When he woke, he made his way back to the tent, and as my luck would have it, just in time to see me saying goodbye to Sakshi. From that moment on, he did not stop asking me very personal questions I was not comfortable answering. Eventually, I told him she gave me her number and that we would see each other when we were both back in Mumbai. He celebrated, probably more than me, teasing me that I now had a girlfriend. I didn't want to get ahead of myself; I wanted to talk to Maa about the weekend and about how I should progress further.

Eventually, Rishi quietened down. I thought I would be able to get some sleep, but my mind was preoccupied with Sakshi. At Mumbai airport, Rishi and I parted ways; I hopped onto the train and sent Maa a message letting her know I was on my way home. The commute on a Sunday was a lot quicker, and finding a place on the bus was a lot easier than usual. I opened my phone and sent a message to Sakshi.

'*I had a nice time this weekend. I'm safely back in Mumbai and looking forward to some coffee.*'

Three dots appeared on my screen instantly, and her reply appeared.

'*Ever the gentleman. I look forward to you asking me for coffee.*'

I smiled at my phone. At my stop, I hopped off and walked to the shop on the corner, picking up a newspaper for Maa and a couple of freshly made samosas. I walked the stairs up to our apartment with a bounce in my step. Inside, I called for Maa, who replied that she was in the kitchen. As I walked in, I found her sitting at the kitchen table, looking tired but welcoming. I put the newspaper down in front of her, kissing her on the forehead, and grabbed two plates from the cupboard.

'And what happened to you,' she said eyeing me, a knowing glint in her eye. I smiled, feigning innocence, and put the plate down in front of her with two samosas before turning back to the counter to put the kettle on.

'Am I to presume you met a girl?'

I turned around; my cheeks hurt from smiling, and I caught myself holding my breath.

'I did, Maa. You remember the girl from the train, the one I told you about? It was her! Her, Maa. She was there this weekend. Rishi says it is serendipity!' I stopped short, embarrassed that I was rambling in the same way that Rishi was on the trip back to Mumbai.

Maa laughed, clearly enjoying my excitement. I placed her tea in front of her and sat down. She encouraged me to tell her everything that happened. I held nothing back, telling her of the drunk woman and how Sakshi used her training as a nurse to help her, how we spoke under the stars, and how Rishi was already calling her my girlfriend.

'I hope you haven't assumed she is your girlfriend yet, Ashray?' She studied me. I sat, mouth open, realising that I had once again gotten too far ahead of myself.

'A woman wants to be courted, Ashray; she wants to know that you will take the time to make her feel special and appreciated before you start putting labels on her.' I nodded, knowing that she was speaking the truth. 'And remember, you do not just court the lady. You court her parents too.' My heart fell into the pit of my stomach remembering the looks of disapproval Sakshi's mother had shot my way. Maa reached her hand across the table to hold mine. 'It will be fine, my boy. Just take it slow and make her feel special.' I smiled and nodded.

While I was gone, Maa hadn't done much, she said; she thought she was coming down with a cold, but insisted on doing my washing from the weekend. After much debate, I relented and handed her my bag before giving back the balance of the money. She raised an eyebrow, and I quickly explained that Rishi had insisted on paying for most of the weekend. With a kiss on the forehead, I went through to my room to prepare for tomorrow morning's workday.

I had two big clients I needed to present portfolios to, and was expecting that, by Friday, I would have them as permanent clients. I wanted to impress this week, to prove that I could come straight out of training and deliver results. As soon as Maa was done in the bathroom with the washing, I hopped into the shower, discarding the grime from the weekend. I laid out my suit for the following day; again, I chose not to wear an outlandish tie. I would wear my flamingos the day after I signed my first permanent client, I told myself.

I lay back in bed, switching on my laptop to perfect my presentations. It wasn't long before sleep called me, and I closed the laptop screen, allowing darkness to take me into dreams of a future where Maa, Sakshi and I lived a happy life.

My second week at BusinessForward saw me sign on three permanent clients. Vihaan came downstairs an hour after the third signed off on my proposal to congratulate me. He was at my desk, singing my praises, when Rishi slid back on his office chair.

'He's not only a genius at work, but also with the women,' he said with a grin. 'Did you know that he managed to meet a woman last weekend and somehow convince her that they could sleep in the same tent!'

Vihaan looked at me; I looked down.

'So, you are quite the Casanova then? When's the first date?' he patted me on the back.

'It's not like this clown here describes it,' I said, embarrassed by Rishi's lack of tact. 'I met her on the train, and we happened to bump into each other this weekend. I intend on asking her out on a date this week.'

Vihaan put his hands up in mock defeat before laughing and saying, 'I'm more interested in why you were sleeping in a tent, but that is a story for another day. I have a board meeting now,' he said, and turned to walk away. 'Hey, Ashray, don't wait too long to ask the girl out. She sounds like a catch, and you wouldn't want some other clown to ask her before you.' He gestured towards Rishi, who clutched his chest and acted wounded.

I laughed, content at the moment. As soon as the elevator bell signalled that Vihaan had left, Rishi clipped me on the back of the head.

'You haven't asked her out yet?' He spoke a little too loudly and I frowned at him. He shook his head before rolling back to his desk. An internal message popped up on my desktop. It was from Rishi.

'*Seeing as you won't answer me—when are you going to ask her out?*'

I replied with an angry face, but internally, I was laughing at my friend. He was muttering something behind me; the familiar roll of his chair wheels made me laugh loudly.

'My phone is flat, and I need to text a friend urgently. Can I use yours?' he asked. I fed in the passcode and handed him my phone.

Opening a new request for a portfolio, I began to formulate a plan to win my next client over. I clicked on their website, taking notes as I scrolled through. From behind me, Rishi punched the air and pushed his chair back a little too hard, crashing into mine. He handed me back my phone with a little too much enthusiasm, and my stomach knotted.

'What did you do?' I whispered.

'You have a date on Friday night with the lovely Sakshi,' he said with a wide grin.

'I what?' I shouted, and the office turned to look at us. Rishi bent over to hide his laughter.

'Take her somewhere nice, okay?' he said as he rolled back to his desk.

I unlocked my phone to check the messages. Sure enough, Sakshi had confirmed for a date on Friday evening. I put my head in my hands, not sure whether I should be angry with Rishi or not. I decided that his temporary step over into my personal space was acceptable before mimicking his earlier behaviour, fist punching the air.

The remainder of the week flew by. I was unable to sign my fourth client, but I was sure that they would commit by early next week. Maa convinced me that expensive dates were not needed; eventually, I decided on a picnic in Hanging Gardens, where we could talk without worrying about distractions.

Arriving at Sakshi's house, I remembered Maa's advice about courting the parents as well as the woman. I did my best to impress her father, but was met with condescending looks from her mother once again. When we boarded the bus, Sakshi took my hand, instinctively knowing that I felt uneasy by her mum's behaviour.

'Ignore my mother, Ashray. She does not understand marrying for love. This is not her way. She will come to accept it eventually,' she said and gave my hand a light squeeze, her eyes filled with compassion. If I was to be honest, I did not hear the rest of what she said after that; my mind fixated on what she had said about love.

'Love?' I repeated, hopeful that I had not misinterpreted what she was saying. She replied with her smile, an expression that I longed to see for more hours of the day than I cared to admit.

'Yes Ashray, love.' She extended her hand and placed it gently on my face. I returned her smile, feeling that it inadequately matched what she had just admitted. My mind, as it always did, took hold, sending me too far into the future, away from the present. A million questions flew around, but I tried, for the remainder of our time on the date, to listen intently to what she said. At the end of the evening, I accompanied her home, despite her protests, and at the front of the building, I lightly kissed her cheek before saying goodnight.

By the time I got home, Maa was sleeping, and the only other person I could speak to was Rishi. I sent him a text telling him how the evening had gone. He replied that it was a bit early to be speaking of love, and although my head agreed with him, my heart told me differently. I couldn't help it; I was falling in love with this woman, and I had no control over it.

Over the next two weeks, Sakshi and I spent almost every evening together. I fell for her, deeper and harder than I had for any woman before her. In fact, I had always been too afraid to let anyone come even near the boundaries I had created for myself. But with Sakshi, all my fears and insecurities vanished.

I was convinced that she was the one I had been waiting my entire life for. We spoke eagerly of the future together. Of how she would complete her studies and of how, finally, we could both live the futures we had always dreamed of. We wanted the same things, and felt passionately about our shared dreams. I felt bad, though, for pushing Rishi away. I tried to apologise, but he insisted that love came first. Underneath it though, I could see that he was hurt.

At the end of the month, I eventually convinced him to come out with me after work, and we caught up with all the news we had missed out on. Sakshi didn't mind, and Maa reminded me that friends were just as important as a girlfriend. Rishi listened intently as I recounted stories about Sakshi, but I tried to make the conversation about him. I will admit, I had missed my friend, missed his laughter and infectious enthusiasm.

When I got home that night, Maa was slumped in her chair in front of the television; she did not look well. I woke her to take her to bed, insisting that we see a doctor the next day. She waved me away, telling me it was just a cold and some extra weight she was carrying. We laughed as I put her to bed, comparing how she used to tuck me in when I was a boy to how I was trying to tuck her in now. I made a mental note to make an appointment with a doctor soon. I would have to ask HR for the day off, but I didn't think it would be an issue. My client portfolio base was strong, especially for someone in their first month; I came into work early, and often worked late at night from home.

I kissed Maa on the forehead and made my way through to my room. Opening my phone, I sent a goodnight message to Sakshi and a thank you to Rishi for being so patient with my budding new romance. Opening the news page on my phone, I was met with the usual social media news. Apparently there was a woman from Mumbai who had become a top 'influencer'. I rolled my eyes, locked my phone and put it on charge.

15

JHANVI

The problem with control is that it is ever-present, exhausting, a game of tug of war that you cannot, even for a moment, loosen your grip on. Letting go, resting, for even a second, means that you have lost control. Sending you home as a loser, or trying with all your might, with all your energy, to regain the advantage; to regain control. The problem with expending energy is that it needs to be replenished; nourishment needs to come from somewhere, from someone.

I'd forgotten that Kavya had a set of keys to my apartment. She walked in while I lay sprawled on the couch. Thankfully, my vodka and energy drink mix was in a mug. Not so thankfully, I'd had no choice but to pour the drink in my coffee mug because the rest of my dishes lay dirty in the sink. It had been two weeks since the music festival, and most of my days were spent replying to messages in my inbox and posting content to my social media. Nights were lonely; I didn't want to be at home at first, in the empty quietness of my apartment. At the pub down the street, I was accepted with open arms; I didn't need to worry about the pitying looks from Kavya, and I certainly didn't need to worry about her comments about my drinking.

I was so engrossed in my profile feed that I didn't hear the door open; my attention was only drawn to her when she spoke.

'My god, Jhanvi! What is all this?' She stood at the doorway to my living room. Boxes were scattered on the floor, some open, some not. Clothing lay strewn over every surface. Under the clothing, makeup and skin products piled high. I had managed to move the supplements and foodstuff to the kitchen yesterday, only because I stood on a chocolate protein bar that burst out of its wrapper and spread sticky brown chocolate all over a denim jacket I still needed to model. I sat up on the couch, not taking my eyes off my phone.

'Brand deals,' I muttered, scrolling through my statistics. Kavya walked through to the kitchen. There was a screech, and then I could hear her curse. I ignored her, concentrating on writing my stats down; next to each of them, I wrote a solution on how to grow the number. My phone was ripped from my hand, and Kavya was standing over me, one hand on her hip.

'There are bugs in your kitchen, Jhanvi. Bugs!' She looked thoroughly unimpressed. 'You cannot live like this; get up. We are cleaning up all of this today.' I protested, telling her I had work to do.

'Jhanvi, you cannot keep up with all of these brands and shoots if your stuff is lying all over the place! You need some order to this chaos or one of these people is going to tell another that you are unprofessional because you don't do as you are asked.' She held up the spoiled denim jacket with an I'm-not-even-going-to-ask look on her face.

Kavya did make sense, and she was right; this sudden growth had gotten the better of me far too quickly. She picked up my coffee cup and took a sniff, curling up her nose. Before she could ask, I told her it was some new natural energy drink I was trying for a company. She marched through to the kitchen, and I heard my newly poured drink being thrown down the sink. Standing up, I stretched and followed her to the kitchen. She was standing over the sink of dishes, shaking her head.

'All right, I'm up. I'll do the dishes if you can dry them and put them away.' She nodded and moved aside so that I could pack the dirty dishes on the counter before filling the sink with hot water.

'Jhanvi, is this about what happened at the music festival?'
She looked around the kitchen at the chaos and mess.

'Nothing happened at the festival, Kavya.' I rolled my eyes,
trying to avoid a conversation I didn't want to have.

'I found you half naked in a stranger's tent, covered in your
own sick and with no recollection of what happened, Jhanvi.'
Her eyes seemed to burn right through me.

'It was nothing, okay? I let loose, got a little out of control.
Nothing bad happened—really. And I learned my lesson,
Kavya. It will never happen again. Trust me.' I gave her a light
hug from behind, trying to avoid her gaze.

She finally nodded and turned back to the dishes. Once
they were done, Kavya grabbed three empty boxes from the
living room. She marked them 'tried', 'to try', and 'donate' with
a capital K after donate, explaining that whatever I did not like
was to be put in that box for her. We sorted through the piles
of food, vouchers and treats, putting them in their relevant
boxes. My head began to pound, and I could feel the slump of
the energy drink wearing off. I headed to the kitchen to make
coffee. Setting out two cups, I put in coffee and sugar. Putting
the coffee back in the cupboard, I saw the bottle of vodka neatly
tucked away behind my flour tin.

'There's a box of protein bars in my bedroom, do you think
you could get them? Might as well get all the foodstuff in their
place,' I said while pouring hot water into the mugs. As soon as
I heard her rummaging through the boxes in my bedroom, I
reached for the vodka. Not measuring out how much I poured,
I quickly replaced the lid and tucked it back in its usual spot.
Being careful to remember whose mug was whose, I placed
Kavya's in its usual spot before joining her in the bedroom.

'Coffee's ready.' I reached over and grabbed the box.

'Where have you been sleeping?' She looked around the
room at the piles of unworn clothes and letters littered across
the bed.

I shrugged. 'Here—I just move everything when it's time to sleep. Come, the coffee will get cold.' I led her out of the room, placed the unopened box of protein bars in the 'to try' box, and sat down to drink my coffee. I would need the caffeine and alcohol if I was going to make it through the day, sorting out the mess that had become my life since the festival.

As we cleared up, Kavya and I spoke about how my following had grown. Eventually she relented, handing me back my phone when I whined that we could film an unboxing. I dressed her in some of my already reviewed clothing, put on an outfit sent by a leading brand, did her makeup and mine, and recorded the unboxing of a new diet sweet that was on the market. Within forty-five minutes, I had enough material to satisfy five new brands.

Happily, I shared how brand deals worked with Kavya, although I wasn't entirely sure how it worked myself. At this point, I felt I was in too deep, that I might drown in my new fame. But failure was not an option. This was my life now, and I would not allow the one thing I had been dreaming of for so long to slip through my fingers because of laziness. After our third cup of coffee, I began to worry that Kavya could smell the alcohol on my breath. I suggested we eat, and she offered to go to the nearby restaurant to get some food. As the door closed behind her, I downed a quarter of the bottle of vodka in my cupboard. I picked up a handful of the appetite-suppressing sweets and chewed through them to mask the smell. When she got back with the takeaway containers, I was buzzed again, the sweets giving me the energy boost I needed. We sat on the living room floor, laughing while we ate and packed clothing and makeup into boxes. Eventually, I was able to convince her that I was tired and wanted to call it a day. Standing up from where we sat on the floor, I swayed.

'If I didn't know better, I would swear you were drunk,' Kavya said, laughing at me. I laughed too, and dismissed my swaying as being lightheaded from getting up so quickly. She picked up her box, promising to return during the week after work. Closing the door behind her, I leaned back. I was drunk and tired. I needed an energy drink to help me get through the night: I needed to edit my work, post for my brands and make sure that my schedule allowed for me to get out and capture some decent shots.

I opened the kitchen cupboard and poured some vodka into my coffee cup, checking my phone to pass the time while the kettle boiled. The content from today was doing well, and some of the brands had replied with positive feedback. There was a club opening in a week, and the owners wanted me to attend. I sent back my standard gushing response, and made a note in my online calendar the way Kavya had shown me. I smiled as the message popped up, saying I would be reminded twelve hours before the event.

'See, you've got this, Jhanvi,' I told myself. Moving to a box of clothing Kavya had marked as urgent, I picked an outfit for the next day. I decided I would go to one of the more popular tourist spots to take photos. Kavya was, of course, working. I squashed down the feelings of loneliness, replacing them with glee as a box marked Nike caught my attention. Inside, a pair of black and gold leopard print sneakers in my size was nestled in the flimsy paper. I closed the box, being careful to replace the paper, and reached for my phone. I hit record, and re-enacted the joy I felt earlier. It felt strange, false; but this was my life now. This is what I had signed up for, and it was worth it. I posted the video to my stories, keeping the photo for the next day so that I didn't bombard my followers with too many sponsored posts.

A familiar sound broke the silence. I looked down at my screen. It wasn't Sunday. Was it? The word Mom stared back at me. I checked the time. Too early to say I was asleep. I sighed and swiped 'accept'.

'Hi, Mom.' I tried to sound as sober as I possibly could. 'Everything okay?'

'Fine, fine. Everything good with you, Jhanvi?'

'Yes,' I replied. 'Sorry I took so long to answer. I must have lost track of time. I didn't realise it was Sunday already.' There was an awkward silence before my mother answered.

'You forgot it was Sunday? That's very strange, Jhanvi. Are you sure everything is all right?'

I rolled my eyes, the familiar feeling of my mother's passive intrusion creeping in.

'I'm good, Mom, really. I have just been quite busy, so—'

She cut me short. 'Mr Pillai at the grocery store showed me your picture on the gossip pages, Jhanvi. They are saying you are India's new big "influencer" girl. Apparently, this is a good thing?'

'I didn't realise,' I admitted to my mother. 'But yes, it is a good thing, Mom.' I sighed.

'Jhanvi, you sound distracted. Do you not think you are working too hard? How about a break? You could come here, to Delhi, spend some time with Dad and me?'

'I just got back from a weekend away with Kavya, but soon Mom.' I made my excuses to cut the conversation short; I couldn't help feeling that my mother was interrogating me. In hindsight, I realised that it was probably my guilt for not phoning her first, but in my defence, I had been working all day. I asked her to convey my love to my dad, promising to call her next weekend. I disconnected the call and grabbed the bottle of vodka. The last thing I remember was scrolling through Puneet's feed; he still wasn't famous, but he was now in a relationship with the girl from the photo. Nausea overtook me as I ran to the bathroom to empty the contents of my stomach. I lay on the bathroom floor, the cool tiles against my face. The room began to spin. I closed my eyes. 'We've all been here,' I thought. 'Haven't we?'

16
ASHRAY

It came as a surprise. I'd had a feeling over the last few weeks that Sakshi was avoiding me, and when we were together, she seemed a little distant. Rishi convinced me that it was just the honeymoon phase coming to an end.

'Your relationship is just settling into a normal pattern now, Ashray. Try to relax,' Rishi said as he handed me a cup of coffee from the café downstairs. 'Soon, you will be discussing wedding plans.' I tried to reciprocate his enthusiasm, but deep down, something felt off. I asked him at our breakfast ritual how I should approach the situation with Sakshi. He insisted I leave it; things would settle eventually. To take my mind off what I felt was my girlfriend's strange behaviour, I ploughed into work. Although I was still new in my position, I had already far surpassed the expectations the company had from me.

But while work was thriving, my relationship seemed to be waning. I tried to squash down my feelings of inadequacy, telling myself I was being paranoid. It was just a lull, a moment in our relationship that would make us stronger. I don't know why, but I kept it from Maa, when she should have been the first person I went to.

Sakshi and I had made plans to meet that night and, as I opened my phone to text her, I told myself tonight would be different.

'Pick you up at 8?'

Her response was almost immediate.

'I'll meet you there.'

My heart sank. Why was I not being allowed to pick her up from her house, as I always did? And then, of course, there was the absence of one important component in her message. No affection. I locked my phone, trying not to think about it. Telling myself I was blowing things out of proportion. That, with her upcoming final exams, Sakshi was just preoccupied, and as soon as she received her results, things would be back to normal.

A calendar reminder flashed up on my screen, 'make Maa's appointment'. I snoozed it until the next day. I needed to deal with Sakshi and my relationship first. Besides, Maa seemed to be on the mend from her cold; she had even lost a little bit of weight after I insisted that she eat a healthy diet. I made a mental note to speak to Maa tomorrow, to ask her if she felt she needed to see a doctor. My work schedule for the next few weeks was pretty full, and I didn't know if I had the time to take a day off, to accompany her to the doctor.

I unlocked my phone again, unable to get rid of the gnawing feeling inside me.

'*Everything all right?*'

I waited, but the three dots didn't appear on my screen. I told myself she was busy studying. At six o' clock, I logged off my work computer and followed Rishi down to the café. We ordered a few light snacks and a cup of coffee; there would not be enough time for me to make the commute home and get back in time to meet Sakshi for our date.

Rishi, too, had a date. He had recently started dating Latika, the woman from the festival. She was newly single after finding her boyfriend in bed with another woman. Rishi, of course, was there to offer her comfort as she went through her breakup. By the end of her mourning period, which wasn't very long, mind you, the two of them were an item. According to Rishi, they were a perfect match. Both enjoyed having fun and being outdoors, rather than sitting at home. She made my friend happy, and I truly enjoyed hearing about their antics. Often, I would find myself longing for the days when Sakshi and I had fun the way the two of them did.

'It's seven-fifteen, Ashray,' Rishi said, pulling me out of my thoughts. 'You better be going, or you're going to be late for Sakshi, and then you really won't be popular.' He slapped me on my back.

I nodded, agreeing that it was time to go before grabbing my jacket that was draped over the back of the chair. I removed my tie, undoing the top button of my light blue work shirt, and popped it into my jacket pocket. Picking up my briefcase, I shook Rishi's hand. Wishing him luck for his date with Latika, I walked out into the night. Monsoon season was over, and the weather was beginning to become cooler, or as cool as a Mumbai night could be. On the ride to our usual meeting spot, I sent Sakshi a message to let her know I was on my way. This time, she did reply; there even seemed to be affection in her tone. I hopped off the bus feeling a little lighter about our meeting and saw her waiting for me outside our usual restaurant. I embraced her and gave her a light peck on the cheek, our usual greeting. I didn't know if I was being paranoid, but I was sure I felt her body stiffen when I touched her.

'Come, let's walk a bit before dinner tonight,' she said, taking my hand. We walked one block down, hand in hand, looking through the stalls, dodging night-time home-goers and beggars. The night air was thick with city smog, but I sensed something was hanging between us as well. On a quieter street, Sakshi turned to me.

'Look, Ashray. There is no easy way to say this. We can't see each other after tonight. I'm sorry.' Her eyes were sad, too sad for a woman who didn't care for her boyfriend.

'I don't understand,' I muttered, unable to tear my eyes away from hers. Tears began to fall from her eyes, and I could see her breathing deeply, trying to control the emotions welling up inside her.

'My parents don't approve, Ashray. This is not what they have in mind for me. I just … I …' she trailed off, trying to control her sobs. I pulled her into me, her head on my chest. I wanted to join her, wanted her to know my sorrow was as great as hers, but I couldn't. My tears seemed stuck in my chest.

'Surely I can explain it to your parents. My Maa can meet them, and we can start talking about getting married. I am sure that, given a chance, they will see that we are a perfect match.' Her sobs became audible; I swallowed down my own.

'It's not that simple, Ashray,' she said, pulling back from me. 'They have already found me a husband. Hell! They have found me three husbands. I just need to choose one.' I recoiled at the thought of her meeting with other men while we were dating.

'I … I just don't understand why you would agree to go out with me, knowing that your parents expected you to marry someone else.'

'I thought if they got to know you, they would see that their arranged marriage plans didn't matter. That, maybe, they would even discuss marriage with your Maa.' She held her composure, trying to explain her logic. I shook my head, feeling deep betrayal. She took my hand and brushed her fingers over my knuckles; her eyes implored me to try and understand.

'I love you, Sakshi,' I whispered.

'I …' There was a catch in her voice. I sensed she wanted to say the words that were so easy for her to say not even a week ago. Instead, she said two words I thought I would never forget. 'I know,' she responded.

As she walked away, I was sure my heart shattered in my chest. I couldn't breathe. Couldn't feel anything other than a rising pain that I thought would consume me. Pushing my way through the couples milling around on the pavements, I hailed a taxi. I couldn't handle the crowds that I knew would be waiting for me on public transport. At the apartment, Maa was sitting on her chair in the living room. She looked at me, her expression changing from enthusiasm to pity the second she saw the sorrow in my eyes. Throwing her arms outwards, she beckoned me to her. Unashamedly, I cried in my mother's arms. I released all the betrayal I felt; all the heartbreak I had held inside while Sakshi had spoken. Eventually, when I could think of no other reasons to cry, I pulled back from her and sat at her feet. I told her what happened, how Sakshi had to decide between three men, none of whom was me. My mother placed her hand on my cheek with a gentle smile.

'Ashray, Sakshi rejecting you is not a sign that you did anything wrong or that you are a bad person. Do you understand?' I nodded, not sure why this was relevant to my situation. 'Sometimes we fall in love with people because we feel time is moving too quickly, but that person may not be the right one. Your life, your pain right now, is just a way to guide you back to the person you are meant to be with. She is one person, Ashray, not every person. You will find the right woman, I promise you.'

I smiled, sure that when the raw emotions subsided, I would understand what she was saying. I kissed her on the forehead, telling her that I needed to sleep. In bed, I plugged my phone in, not bothering to check for messages. I buried my head in my pillow and cried. When Sakshi walked out of my life, she took a part of me—a part that I felt was vital to survive. Like waking from a deep sleep to find that you no longer have your legs. That you need to relearn everything you thought that you knew.

When my alarm went off the next morning, I didn't want to get out of bed. I rolled over and pressed the snooze button. My head ached, but not as much as the dull ache in my heart. There was a quiet knock on the door before Maa walked into my room. She sat on the corner of my bed, running her fingers through my hair the way she used to when I was a young boy. I sat up in bed, knowing she was going to suggest I take the day off work. The truth was, I didn't want to get up today, but I had a big presentation I couldn't miss. Swinging my legs out of bed, I kissed my Maa on the head. Telling her I was fine, I walked to the bathroom. I washed my face with cold water, trying to bring down the swelling under my eyes.

In the kitchen, Maa had made me tea in a flask to take on the way to work. Instead of the train, I took the bus that day; I couldn't risk running into Sakshi. I hung around outside when I arrived at the office, trying to avoid Rishi. I pulled out my phone, opening the news page to distract myself. A hand landed on my shoulder; a hot cup of coffee seemed to hover in mid-air. Rishi came into view, and the look on his face told me he already knew about what happened the night before.

'You okay?' He looked at me with the same knowing look that Maa gave me.

'How did you know?'

'Your Maa texted me this morning, asking me to look out for you today. I put two and two together after that.' He lowered his gaze.

'How do you date a man knowing you can never be with them?' I asked, a little more angrily than I should have. '*How*, Rishi? She played with my heart for months!'

Rishi nodded, listening to me without interrupting. Unlike Maa, he didn't offer advice. Instead, he listened until I couldn't talk anymore. Then, finally, he spoke. 'You're going to be fine, Ashray. I won't tell you she didn't deserve you because she was a special girl, but there will be other special girls, and one day you will find one that is prepared to fight for your love.'

Finally, what Maa had said the previous night made sense. I stood up from the bench, and with Rishi's strength next to me, I got through the day.

17

JHANVI

Destruction. The kind that only you can prevent or the type only your behaviour can provoke. A downward spiral, an annihilation you could have prevented if you decided to. If you chose to take a second to breathe, to think, but you didn't; you thought you couldn't, and now, in the aftermath, all that is left is wreckage.

I woke up on the bathroom floor, shivering. It wasn't cold, but I couldn't stop my body's reaction to whatever it was trying to eliminate from its system. I lifted myself off the floor; my head protested as loudly as my stomach. I put my hand on the basin, steadying myself as I waited for the room to stop spinning. I turned the tap and washed my face with ice-cold water before slowly walking to the kitchen to make myself a cup of coffee. As the kettle boiled, I opened the cupboard. There was no alcohol left, but that was not what I was after. I needed aspirin for my head. The black coffee would take care of my stomach.

Sitting in the living room with the piping hot brew in my hands, I opened my phone and watched the screen fill with hearts. I posted my first photo of the day, remembering to add the required hashtags. My follower count was growing faster than even I had anticipated, and while it seemed I had everything I dreamed of, I couldn't help feeling that my life was falling apart.

Finishing my coffee, I walked to the bathroom and switched the shower on; I tested the temperature before getting in. The warm water soothed my stiff muscles. My mind went over the plans for the week, mentally noting each outfit I would wear for my clients. I had the club opening on Friday, something I couldn't miss, and as much as I wanted Kavya with me, I didn't feel like listening to her nagging me about how much I was drinking or how little I was eating.

Back in the kitchen, I took out a protein bar and bit into it, oblivious to how terrible it actually tasted. I threw the wrapper in my bin, not wanting to deal with Kavya's disapproval again.

I did my makeup and dressed for the day's shoot before leaving my apartment, bag in hand. Outside, the city smells assaulted my stomach. I turned left at the top of my street and walked into the nearest pharmacy. Off the shelves, I picked up an antacid, and from the corner of my eye, a packet of old-fashioned dieting pills caught my attention. I remembered stories from when I was in school about how other students would take them to stay awake to study. I grabbed two boxes and placed them on the counter along with the antacid, ignoring the dirty looks from the woman serving me. Two shops down, I went into the local market to buy a bottle of water and a replacement bottle of vodka. I slipped the vodka into my bag and hailed a taxi.

The day was near perfect. At the Hanging Gardens, the majestic buildings and carefully pruned shrubbery contrasted against the blue sky. I couldn't help but feel the entire moment was surreal. I pulled out my selfie stick, carefully placed my phone in the allotted space, and began taking photos. I scrolled through the photos and was satisfied with the results. I selected one I liked and posted the picture for my followers to enjoy. The only one I looked happy in.

I looked around, happy couples and friends seemed to be enjoying the relatively mild Mumbai weather. At that moment, I felt lonely; like no one truly understood. That amongst all the noise, all the popularity, I stood alone. I pulled out my phone to send Kavya a message before deciding against it. I walked back to the main street, hoping to find a taxi home as quickly as possible. All around me, people walked with purpose.

'You're getting in?' A voice from a nearby cab summoned me. I nodded and ran to the waiting taxi. Closing the door behind me, I slumped back in my seat. I couldn't get rid of the nagging feeling inside me: What was my purpose? Why was I here? To influence people into living the kind of life I lived? I opened my phone in search of a comment, any comment, from a young girl who needed guidance, but when I found one, I didn't know what to type. I locked my phone and leaned my head back on the seat, hoping I would get home soon. But the taxi ride home was slow—traffic congested the streets. They reflected the congested thoughts in my mind.

Outside my apartment building, I pushed past the local begging community, annoyed that they would block my path. I was irritated and needed to get inside. My hands shook as I tried to get my key in the door, my palms were damp with sweat, and my head was pounding. Finally the key turned in the lock; pushing the handle down, I burst into the apartment and slammed the door behind me. I tried to steady my breathing; my hands shook with such ferocity I thought I would drop my phone. I ran through to the kitchen and splashed water on my face, pausing to breathe deeply. I sat at the kitchen table. Reaching into my bag, I grabbed the bottle of vodka and, hands shaking, I opened the lid and took a swig. The clear liquid hit my stomach like fire, and I resisted the urge to be sick. I took another swig.

'You're just tired,' I told myself. Bottle in hand, I made my way through to the living room and lay on the white, leather, double-seater sofa Kavya and I had picked out when I moved into this apartment. A wave of tiredness washed over me. A quick nap wouldn't hurt. I reached over to grab my phone; over a hundred emails awaited my reply. I groaned. Opening my bag, I rummaged around for the pharmacy packet. Two pills in hand, I took a deep breath.

'It's just this one time, Jhanvi. To get through today.' I put the pills in my mouth and swallowed hard. The next four hours were a blur. I felt fantastic. The pills didn't make me feel different, 'hyper' as the kids in school would say. I felt balanced, the way I felt before Puneet. By seven that night, I had finished my emails and posted two additional photos. My follower count was rising steadily, and my entire month was planned out. Standing to make myself a coffee, I felt the familiar spinning feeling that I had experienced in the morning. I grabbed another protein bar out of the cupboard. Turning around, I let out a scream.

'My god, Kavya! You almost gave me a heart attack!'

'I've been trying to get hold of you the whole day,' she shot back. 'If you used your phone for anything other than social media, you would know I was coming over with dinner.'

'Actually, I used it to answer my emails and put all my commitments in my calendar today.' I was very aware of my childish, belligerent attitude, but at that moment, I didn't care. The room began to spin. Putting my hands on the counter, I steadied myself.

'Are you drunk, Jhanvi?' The look on her face changed from anger to concern.

I searched my mind, trying to remember where I had left the vodka bottle. In my bag, I put it back in my bag. This was salvageable.

'No, Kavya,' I shot back, surprising myself at the venom in my voice. I softened my tone. 'No. I just haven't been sleeping well, and if you must know, I think I'm coming down with something.'

'I'm worried about you, Jhanvi. You're so stuck in this,' she gestured towards the phone in my hand, 'you've forgotten that real people exist. People who actually care about you!' I didn't want to have this conversation with her. Not now, anyway. It didn't feel like a fight, but she was relentless, pushing me for answers I didn't have. What she said was true, and the truth hurt. It cut deep. The rage built inside me.

'Listen!' I yelled back. 'I have told you this before. I do not need someone policing my every mood, and I do not need a mother! You land up here uninvited, under the guise of friendship, but actually you're just here to check on me or to bum your next box of free stuff, and I don't mind, Kavya. Really, I don't, as long as you keep your damned opinions to yourself!'

She took a step back. I saw the pain I had inflicted on her, but I couldn't stop. The rage that had been building inside me was on the surface, and like a volcano, lying dormant for hundreds of years, nothing could stop the destruction that followed.

'Jhanvi, you're drunk. Please,' she pleaded with me.

'Oh, what? Now that I dare speak back, you change your attitude?' I took a step forward; lifting my finger, I stuck it in her face. 'You are a freeloading witch who loves nothing more than to cause me misery! You couldn't wait to prove to me that Puneet was cheating, and you cannot wait to save your poor miserable friend from her next misfortune. But you know what, Kavya? I don't need you. I don't need your sympathy, and I certainly don't need your bitchy attitude arriving in my house every day to force-feed me crap so that you can feel better about getting fat!'

My breathing was out of control, rage driving me to say things I didn't mean. Things that had never even crossed my mind. Venom taking over my words and twisting everything into something cruel.

Kavya turned around and, without saying a word, she put the food on the kitchen counter. I saw her pause for a moment, perhaps to say something or perhaps taking in one last moment with her, now ex, best friend. She walked out of the room. I was sure I heard her place her keys on the front side table before the familiar click of the front door closing permeated the silence. I walked through to the living room and grabbed the bottle of vodka from my bag. I pushed out two pills, put them in my mouth, and downed as much of the bottle as my stomach would permit before I choked.

Unlocking my phone, I scrolled through my comments; they were filled with young girls telling me how my life was wonderful, how they envied me. Pacing the room, I read them out loud, like a madwoman. I repeated the opinions of people who didn't even know me. I spoke into the nothingness of my apartment. Bottle in hand, I paced, I don't know for how long, until I could no longer contain the rage.

'My life is perfect!' I screamed, as I launched the bottle across the room. The bottle exploded on impact and there were glass shards everywhere. I sank to my knees; hands on my face, I breathed. I needed to control this one thing, control my breathing. It took me a moment before I could stand up. I walked to my kitchen to grab the broom and a dustpan. Sweeping up the mess, a shard of glass cut my finger. Crimson blood pooled on my skin.

'Quite the mess,' I muttered to myself as I robotically continued to clean up. No emotion left inside me. Only control.

18
ASHRAY

Do you know the feeling? That dull ache that you seem to carry around with you after someone has broken your heart. For weeks, I walked around in a stupor, convincing anybody who would listen that I was fine, that Sakshi's betrayal had not devastated me. The truth was that, some days, I did not want to get out of bed, not understanding why I was not worthy of love. I would later understand that no matter how much love Maa showered on me, the feelings of betrayal and abandonment from being left on the steps of an orphanage still played heavily on my psyche. I felt neglected, discarded for something or someone better; that no matter what I did to better my life, it wasn't enough. Maa and Rishi tried to reach out; they tried to distract and guide me. But I found myself wallowing, unable to pull myself out of the depths of my own self-loathing.

'Eat something, Ashray,' Maa said as she pushed a plate of food closer to me.

'I'm fine.' I pushed it back away from me.

'You have to eat something, Ashray,' she said insistently, pushing the food back within my reach. I knew she meant well, but I was tired of everyone telling me how I should feel, react or move on from Sakshi. She hadn't even bothered to text, not once, not even to ask how I was.

'I said I am fine!' I banged my hands on the table, causing Maa to jump in her seat. I pushed my chair back and stormed out of the kitchen and apartment, slamming the front door behind me.

Mumbai nights were busy; those who tried to escape the heat during the day loitered around when the sun went down.

The owner of the shop at the corner greeted me with a smile while he tried to thrust a free sheet newspaper in my hand. I waved it away, not interested in speaking to anyone. My feet pounded the ground as I picked up pace. I felt that it matched the rhythm of my heart, which threatened to explode in my chest. I don't know how long I walked for, or why my mind insisted on replaying Sakshi's words.

'I know'—such a strange thing to answer when someone tells you they love you, but that's what she had said. She didn't fight for me, didn't care enough to show her parents that I was not garbage to be discarded. How dare she play with my heart the way she had?

'How dare she?' I shouted.

'Are you all right there, beta?' An old man approached me, hands outstretched. I wanted to escape; from the pain, from my failure and from my mind, which would not stop tormenting me with the could-have-been, if Sakshi had fought for me. And now, I was pushing away the one person who had never turned her back on me, the woman who did fight for me. Guilt rose thick and heavy in my throat as I thought of Maa's face when I left the house. I turned on my heels and ran home, irrational fear gripping me. I was sure that I would return and the locks would be changed. Abandoned and discarded because of my actions. When I got back, the door was unlocked, and Maa had retreated to bed. I knocked on her door, tentatively, but she did not answer. I found a pen and paper, scribbled a note that I knew would provoke comments on my handwriting, and propped it up on the kitchen counter.

Wake me if you are up before me. I am sorry, Maa.

Collapsing in bed, I hoped that the loop circling in my head would be broken, played out. I needed to sleep, needed to rid my thoughts of Sakshi, but it was impossible while my mind fought back. I opened my bedroom window wide, begging the noises of the city to distract me from the insanity my mind forced me into. The day ended the same way it began, with a dull ache in my chest and the heaviness of dreams shattered.

The sound of traffic stirred me from my sleep. The first light of day teasing me out of my rest, I rolled over to check the time. Eight hours, that was more sleep than I had had since … I stopped myself from starting the day with thoughts of her. In the kitchen, Maa was making tea. I walked up to her, ready to be apologetic.

'Morning, Maa.' I reached over to kiss her on the forehead the same way I had done since I was tall enough to. Sad eyes looked back at me, and I couldn't hold back the flood. Tears that had been building for weeks flowed freely, like they were bursting through the wall of a dam. 'I'm sorry,' I managed, before laying my head on her shoulder, unashamed of my tears.

'My boy,' she lifted my head from her shoulder, a hand rubbing my back in comfort. 'I know it hurts, but you cannot hurt those who are supporting you through this. What good would a crutch be if you kept knocking it until it breaks? It doesn't matter what this says,' she patted me on the forehead with a frail, thin finger, 'there will always be hope.' I smiled at her, accepting her analogy for what it was.

'I want to take you shopping today,' I said, stroking her cheek. 'We can go to the market, get some food for the house and something nice for you.' She smiled back at me, and I knew I was forgiven. Maa never punished me for feeling anything. She understood that somewhere, deep inside of me, something was broken; something she had spent her whole life trying to fix. But I was the crutch that was continually knocked, and piece by piece, I felt that I was being broken.

'Let me hold your arm please,' I said, grabbing Maa's arm as she moved to step over a broken fruit crate. She slapped my hand away, scowling like a toddler preparing to throw a tantrum.

'Will you stop grabbing me, Ashray! I am old, not disabled!'

'You will be disabled if you keep stopping me from helping you.' I reached out to her again. She swung her shopping back at me wildly, showing me that I had pushed her too far. 'Can we at least walk arm in arm?' I grinned at her, trying to deploy Rishi's disarming tactics. She smiled back, looping her arm in mine.

'You see, Ashray? Compromise.' I loved how my Maa always seemed to find a teachable moment in life. How her analogies sometimes didn't make sense, but the intentions were always pure.

'Look at these people Ashray, their noses in their phones.' She motioned towards two women walking towards us; they were focused on the phones in their hands, and not talking to each other.

'In my day, before these things came out, we were forced to talk to each other, that is why arranged marriages worked.' I nodded, not quite understanding what she was saying. 'You couldn't hide behind those things, Ashray. You spoke about how you felt.' I didn't want to talk about relationships, after successfully getting through the day without too many thoughts of Sakshi's rejection.

'I don't know how relationships can work today with all of the outside distractions. While you and I have been talking, those two girls haven't once looked up or acknowledged that other people are around them. They are together, but they could not be further apart.' I squeezed her arm, searching for something to distract her from her train of thought. My heart was still too sensitive to explain to Maa in-depth how I felt for Sakshi or how deeply her rejection had affected me. Thinking about her, about what she had done, brought the familiar feeling of pressure in my chest. I guided Maa towards a stall where brightly coloured pots hung from a white rope.

'What do you think of these?' I asked her, hoping that she would change the subject. 'We could put them on the shelf in the kitchen to bring in some colour?' She nodded thoughtfully before answering.

'If you don't mind, I would prefer those roses over there.' She pointed towards cardboard-bound bunches of crimson and yellow roses. I smiled. She knew that, before Sakshi had dropped the news on me, I was looking for a new place where all of us could live together happily once she had graduated, and that I continued to distract myself with pictures of dream homes. The stairs to our third-floor apartment were beginning to become a problem for Maa and, sooner rather than later, I would need to find a place where there was an elevator she could use.

I patted her arm, and we walked over to the flowers. I watched her face as she breathed in the scent of a bunch of crimson roses. Looking up at the stall owner, I gestured that we would take two.

Arm in arm, I walked with Maa; no more conversations about Sakshi were had. Instead, we spoke about where she would like to live when we moved, and what we would get in the market to make it our home.

19

JHANVI

Three days without Kavya. Have you ever gone for days without your lifeline? I hated to admit it, but I missed her. Missed her visits and her random messages through the day. It didn't bother me during the day, but at night, in the solitude of my apartment, I realised that I was completely alone, other than the strangers who wished they had my life.

I was busy, though, and finally in control of what I was doing, although there was no routine. I had the club opening on Friday night, and no one to take with me. I had to take someone—I couldn't be that woman who seemed desperate and alone—but there was no way that Kavya would say yes. I wasn't even sure she would accept an apology from me yet.

Unlocking my phone, I scrolled through my direct messages, searching for a young up-and-coming influencer. Perhaps I could turn my loneliness into a PR opportunity? A message caught my eye. I had that moment of morbid curiosity, when logic tells you not to get involved, yet, somehow, you end up doing so anyway. Latika's message was a jumble of gratification for our newfound friendship, sorrow and anger over her breakup with Gaurav, and admiration for the amount of work I was receiving. Contemplating the drama it could bring for only a second, I hit reply.

'He's not worth it, anyway! You busy later today?'

I wasn't even sure if Latika would be awake. It was three in the morning, but the energy drink and vodka were still coursing through my veins, doing the job I requested of them. It wasn't long before Latika's reply came through. She had been at a party earlier that night, and was making her way home.

Perhaps I should invite her to the club opening? She liked a good party, was relatively well behaved and full of energy. At least I wouldn't have a constant eye watching me, judging my behaviour. I lay on the bed and closed my eyes, trying to get the sleep that I knew I desperately needed. But it wouldn't come. My mind played tricks on me, willing me to rid myself of the guilt that was building inside after losing my temper with Kavya. But my stubbornness was deep-rooted, and I fought the feeling.

'No more emotion, Jhanvi; only control,' I told myself in the darkness. I repeated it over and over again, until my bedroom turned orange and the sun burned through the darkness. I closed my eyes, knowing that my alarm would go off in two hours. Ignoring the burning hunger pangs, I finally fell asleep.

I jolted awake, sure that I had heard someone in my apartment. Sitting bolt upright in my bed, I looked around. The room spun, and my head throbbed. There was a knocking sound. Why was I finding it so difficult to orient myself? I swung my legs out of bed and fought the rising nausea in my stomach. I reached for my phone, squinting my eyes as the blue screen came to life.

'Shit!' I cursed; I had slept through the alarm. I grabbed a hair tie and loosely pulled my hair away from my face, realising where the banging was coming from. I unlocked the front door and shouted that it was open as I dashed to the bathroom. Latika walked into my apartment, confused on seeing me walking down the passage.

'Am I early?'

'No,' I shouted back. 'I slept through my alarm. Put the kettle on, won't you?' I walked into the bathroom. Closing the door behind me, I turned the tap on to mask the sound of what I knew was coming. Leaning over the toilet, I emptied the contents of my stomach. Hours-old alcohol burned my throat with every heave. I flushed and sprayed the bathroom with a room freshener. I quickly brushed my teeth and applied some makeup before I headed out to Latika in the kitchen. She was leaning against the counter, phone in hand, and a big smile on her face.

'New guy?' I asked, while I took out the mugs for the coffee.

'Is it that obvious?' She smiled. 'And this one treats me right! Three sugars please, a bit of a rough night,' she said, winking at me, insinuating that I should know how she felt.

'So, I was thinking,' I stirred the freshly made coffee and placed it in front of her, 'I have this club opening on Friday; do you want to come with me?'

She clapped her hands in excitement.

'Yes, of course!'

'Okay, so let's go to the market today, see if there's anything you like, and I can decide on your outfit.' She eyed me, and I wondered if I had overstepped.

'Are you sure? I mean, wouldn't you rather take someone who has a bigger following?' I couldn't tell if she was being sarcastic or not. I missed Kavya, missed knowing exactly how to read her reactions.

'I didn't mean to offend you, Latika, I just …' I trailed off, trying to find the words that would help her understand what I didn't. 'I like to dress people up. It's always been my thing. You know, take their style and elevate it to the next level?' She burst out laughing. This woman has far too much energy for this early in the morning, I thought.

'No offence was taken,' she said, lifting her hands in a gesture that was a little too much like Gaurav. 'I would love to accompany you, and I would love to have you dress me. It's just that I'm a little short on cash. Moving out of Gaurav's and into my own place has knocked me a little bit, and I don't have much savings to spend on new outfits.'

'Oh please,' I said, shaking my head at her, 'as long as you aren't insisting on Louis Vuitton, I have you covered.' She grinned at me.

'Right,' I announced. 'Let me get dressed, and we will hit the market.' I walked out of the room, shouting for her to make herself comfortable.

I had a quick shower and slid on a pair of ripped jeans, a gold top and my sponsored Nike sneakers. Large gold hoops adorned my ears, and a pair of leopard print sunglasses finished the look. From my bag, I took two pills, forcing them down with the left-over mix that was next to my bed. The taste was awful, but I needed the energy to get through the day with Latika. Speaking of, she was draped over my sofa when I walked back into my living room. Nose buried in her social media, she was scrolling through Gaurav's feed. I grabbed her phone from her.

'Don't do that,' I admonished her, 'don't make him out to be anything other than a lying, cheating, man-whore. Latika. He's not worth your time.' She looked at me, wide-eyed.

'Man-whore?' She burst out laughing and, clicking on his latest picture with a girl, she typed out the words before hitting 'post'. I gasped at her brashness, not sure whether what she had done was brave or stupid. It was going to be a long day, I thought, before joining in her laughter.

The taxi ride to the market was quieter than I expected. Latika busied herself with messages to her friends while I took photos and videos to add to my archive of social media posts so that I always looked busy. At the market, I searched for locations, taking photos against backdrops using the various stalls and the rich colours of the busy market.

'Jhanvi! Look at this dress. What do you think?'

'Yeah,' I replied, not looking up from my screen. Something strange was happening with my stats, and I didn't know what it was.

'You didn't even look,' she whined. I lifted my head and nodded, trying to seem interested. In hindsight, I should have paid more attention, considering she was going to accompany me to the club opening.

'It's great, Latika, really,' I said, smiling convincingly. 'We'll add some accessories, and the outfit will be perfect.' I handed her the money to pay for whatever it was she wanted; I still hadn't really seen what it was. I could deal with it if it were hideously ugly. There was nothing ugly enough that some good accessorising couldn't fix. Wandering over to the vegetable stalls, I lifted my phone and smiled brightly, trying to portray that I had time for everyday activities as well as being a social media guru.

Latika ambled next to me, trying to make conversation, but I was too involved in what was happening on my screen. I just couldn't shake the feeling that something was wrong. We called a taxi back to my apartment, and for the first time that day, I put my phone away. I had plenty of material to use over the next week as fillers between promotional posts; my numbers were growing, and I couldn't pinpoint the reason I felt so uneasy. Perhaps I just needed a drink and something to eat. I had enough fruits and vegetables to feed an army; healthy lifestyles were trending, and I wanted to give the impression that I had also subscribed to being healthy. I turned to Latika, who was staring thoughtfully out the window, clutching her black plastic packet.

'Show me your dress, then?' I felt a bit bad for ignoring her the whole day, and I couldn't afford to have her sulking. If she refused to come to the club opening, there was literally no one else I could ask. Enthusiastically, she pulled out the dress. I nodded my head in approval; it was a good choice for her small frame, and with a little bit of my special touch, she would look lovely.

'So, tell me about this new guy in your life.'

She clapped her hands in glee. 'Do you remember the shirtless guy who was bringing us shots at the Goa Music Festival?'

I nodded, although I had to admit that I would not recognise him if I saw him right then.

'He is such a gentleman,' she said giddily. She recounted their dates and how he kept in touch with her throughout the day without making her feel like she was his possession. That was one thing Latika and I had in common—we were both once owned by Gaurav. Both dictated to, possessed and eventually discarded by him. At that moment, I realised something: I didn't know if I liked her and if she was someone I would normally be friends with, but she and I were connected by the pain another human being had inflicted on us. Bound by Gaurav, a man we wished we could forget but knew we could not.

'That's so great,' I said to her. Handing back her dress, I gave her hand a light squeeze, not knowing why the feeling of another person's skin touching mine made me want to flee and cry.

20

ASHRAY

The feeling of pressure on my chest was easing up. It had been weeks since Sakshi had broken up with me, and I thought that I had worked through my feelings. Work was going well, and Rishi's relationship kept me entertained. Swearing off love for a little while seemed to suit me, and I even found myself smiling spontaneously again. I had learned that I needed to stop pushing down how I felt, that the emotions welling up inside me needed to be released, and if I refused them, denied them the right to be felt, they would manifest in ways that would destroy me. Vihaan showed concern, saying that I was working too hard, trying to distract myself from my feelings. I rubbished his claims, insisting that I was working to my goal of finding a place where Maa no longer needed to climb stairs.

'Ashray.' The familiar sound of chair wheels rolling broke my train of thought. 'I sent you a mail. Look at that place!' I navigated to my email and opened Rishi's message which had the subject line 'perfect'. Half expecting a joke, I sat back in my chair, trying to stifle a sigh. I was greeted with a picture of a two-bedroom apartment in the neighbourhood I wanted; the building was new and had an elevator.

'What do you think?' Rishi grinned.

I turned to him. 'It's beautiful—and there are no stairs.'

'You haven't seen the best part! Scroll down.' I ran my finger over the mouse as pictures of the idyllic apartment filled my screen. From the living room, sliding doors opened on to a balcony. My mouth curled into a grin that matched Rishi's. Quickly, I looked at the price. It was well within my budget; how was that possible? As usual, he read my thoughts.

'It's a friend's investment property. He doesn't want it standing open; he told me that if I could find a good tenant, he would keep the price reasonable.'

'But don't you want it?' I asked him. He let out a laugh that was probably too loud for the office.

'What am I going to do with two bedrooms and an apartment that size, Ashray?' He had a point. His relationship with Latika was going well, but they weren't serious yet.

'I'll take it,' I said impulsively. 'Do you think we can see it tonight?'

Rishi pulled a set of keys out of his pocket and smiled. He had known I would love the place. Opening my phone, I sent Maa a text.

'Getting off work early. Have a surprise for you; please be ready at 6—we're going out.'

'So, we go and see it with my Maa, and then you come with us for dinner after?'

'Sounds great,' he replied, rolling back to his desk.

Leaving the office early, I hopped onto a bus back to my apartment. There was a spring in my step for the first time in a long while as I ran up the stairs to our apartment. Soon we wouldn't need to do this anymore; Maa would have the freedom to come and go as she wanted. She would have a little balcony garden where she could sit in the morning, drinking her tea.

'Ashray,' she called as I walked into the house.

'I'm here Maa, are you ready to go?'

'Aren't you going to have something to drink before we go?' She popped her head out of the kitchen.

'Rishi is meeting us there, we will have plenty of time afterwards.' I locked arms with her and led her out of the kitchen. She smiled at me lovingly, confusion and delight written on her face, but I knew she didn't want to spoil my excitement at surprising her. Holding her arm as we went down the stairs, knowing that she was straining, I couldn't help but allow myself to be truly happy. I might not have Sakshi by my side, but one of my dreams was being fulfilled. I was earning well, and having a home like the one we were going to see would help in finding me a wife. If my heartbreak had taught me anything, it was that status still mattered when it came to marriage. If I could prove that I was a reliable provider, there was more chance that I would be accepted.

In the taxi ride to the apartment, Maa teased me for clues about where we were going.

'Look at this beautiful market,' I said, pointing out of the window. Early evening traffic was congested, which would normally irritate me, but today it allowed us time to see which shops and areas Maa would be able to explore while I was at work. The driver stopped outside the building. I helped my Maa out of the taxi and paid him. At the door, Rishi waited for us, his normal grin on his face. He greeted Maa and she pulled him into a warm embrace.

'What do you think?' He opened his arms wide, turning in a half-circle.

'I don't know what this is,' she responded playfully.

'Come.' I held her arm as Rishi buzzed us into the building. The front lobby was tiled in light grey, and four new silver elevators lined either side of an indoor rock garden. It smelled clean, unaffected by the pollution outside. Rishi reached for the button on the elevator. It opened instantly.

'This is fancy,' Maa said and smiled. 'I hope you boys aren't taking me for dinner? I already have food prepared at home.'

'Going up,' Rishi said, and pressed the button for the tenth floor. The elevator climbed swiftly and silently up to our destination. The doors opened with a ding, and I led Maa out by the arm into a passage that was decorated in much the same way the downstairs lobby was. Automatic passage lights switched on, and Rishi stepped back, giving me a knowing wink.

We opened the apartment door, and in front of us lay a sprawling open plan living room and dining room area. Glass sliding doors offered an amazing view of Mumbai, although no city sounds could be heard. Maa walked into the apartment, mouth open. She turned left into the kitchen and ran her hands over the granite countertops. I took in her face, wide-eyed and in awe of what she was seeing, but still confused as to what it meant. Rishi slid the doors open, inviting us outside to the balcony. We followed eagerly; for a moment, I couldn't believe this was my life. While she admired the view, I walked back into the apartment to see the rest of it. The main bathroom was on the left of a corridor, and it had no view. The two bedrooms had sliding doors that opened out onto two small balconies. I poked my head around the door and called them over to where I stood.

'Look at these tiles, Ashray,' Maa gasped. 'This is posh!'

'Isn't it, Maa? And look here.' I opened a door that concealed a private bathroom. She put her hands to her mouth to conceal her shock.

'I thought this could be your bedroom,' I said. I swallowed down a familiar lump in my throat, knowing that tears wanted to come; from happiness, this time.

'What?' Maa shouted.

'This is our new home, Maa. No more stairs, no more being inside all day. You can even have some plants in the balconies, if you want.'

'Can we afford this, Ashray?' She looked at me with concern. I walked over to her, love in my eyes, and I wrapped my arms around my Maa.

'I can afford it, Maa; you don't have to worry anymore.' She hugged me tightly, and I thought I heard her swallowing back her tears. At the time, I was completely aware of how much this woman had sacrificed for me; of how much more she was willing to do for me to live my dreams; and I loved her for it. But it was my turn to look after her. To finally have the life she deserved, after so much hardship.

'So, you like it?' I asked her, hopeful that she wouldn't try to talk me out of my dream. She placed her hand on my cheek, dark eyes staring back at me.

'I love it, my boy.' She took my hand as we walked back outside to take in the views together in quiet harmony.

'We can put a little coffee table out here for you, Maa,' I broke the silence. 'You can read your newspaper in some sun in the morning, and maybe, in the afternoon, you could do a little gardening.' She nodded thoughtfully. 'Can you imagine having dinner out on the balcony together?' I grinned.

'I cannot wait to cook for us in the kitchen.' She burst out laughing with excitement.

'So, are you taking it then?' Rishi interrupted our chatter.

'Definitely! When can I sign the papers?'

He smiled at me. 'We'll sort it out tomorrow. Tonight, we have your Maa's delicious food to enjoy.' Rishi smiled at Maa, who melted as she usually did around him.

On the cab ride home, the three of us spoke about when and how we would bring our furniture to the apartment. To begin with, the apartment would be sparsely furnished, but it wouldn't be like that forever. Our entire apartment now could fit into the living room of the new place, but I didn't want to put us under financial pressure. We could furnish it slowly over the next few months. I made a mental note to get the colourful pots we had seen at the market for Maa. That way, when we moved in, they would be waiting for her. Rishi had grand ideas of dinner parties out on our small balcony, which both Maa and I laughed at. I have never been one of those people who enjoyed partying until late at night.

When the taxi arrived outside our apartment, Rishi and I helped Maa up the stairs. Inside the apartment, the aromas of her prepared food enveloped us, and my stomach protested loudly.

'That stomach of yours has a mind of its own,' Rishi said and burst out laughing.

'My boy has always had a good appetite,' Maa replied. 'Surprisingly, he stays this thin.'

Rishi and I hung our suit jackets up while Maa lit the stove to heat the vegetable korma that was torturing my senses. Maa busied herself over the pot while Rishi made jokes about finding a wife that could cook as well as my Maa. I watched the two of them, taking in the moment. My breakup with Sakshi was tough, but as much as I didn't want to hear it from Maa, she was right—the pain does pass, even if it felt like it never would. I would smile again, and I would feel genuinely happy again. Life was fleeting, and people would come and go, but our happiness was ultimately our responsibility. Letting go of Sakshi, of the pain she caused me, was difficult. But ultimately, when the time was right, happiness found me again. Love, in its purest form, filled my home this evening; nothing could have been more perfect. And as I sat at the table, watching my best friend and my Maa, I felt that life was worth living once again. I was not waste that Sakshi had discarded. She was merely a product of her upbringing, and I felt sorry for her, that she would never get to experience what we had in this beautiful moment.

21

JHANVI

I had bitten off more than I could chew with Latika. We've all experienced that feeling; that moment when it becomes painfully obvious that you have made a mistake, but it is impossible to rectify it. This was one of those moments. Latika was rummaging through my perfectly coordinated makeup drawers, searching for the perfect 'lippy', as she put it. My stomach turned with every item that was taken out of its place and not returned. I missed Kavya; she would never do this. I had been thinking about messaging her the previous day, but had finally decided against it. I thought I would give her more time to cool down. But watching Latika gleefully stomping through my personal space drove me to pick up my phone and make contact with the person that had been missing for too long in my life.

'I am really sorry; please can we talk.'

I waited for the three dots to immediately appear on my screen as they always had before, but they never came. Locking my phone, I groaned loudly at Latika's enthusiasm.

'Did you say something?' she said as she applied entirely too much foundation.

'Do you want a drink?' I asked her, trying to salvage the situation and knowing that I needed something to calm my nerves. I had run out of diet pills, and the woman at the pharmacy was beginning to become suspicious. For a while, I would have to stick to vodka and energy drinks to keep my energy levels up.

'Yes, please,' she sang from my dresser. I walked to the kitchen and poured her a single and myself a generous amount of vodka, splitting the energy drink between the two of us. I walked back into the room, feeling like my body was a heavy, lifeless weight I had to drag around.

'Here,' I said as I placed her drink in front of her, 'let me help you.' I reached for a sponge to blend her foundation and got to work on the rest of her face. When I was done with her, she examined herself in the mirror and squealed. I almost choked on my drink at the high-pitched sound.

'You're jumpy,' she said, looking at me with what I thought was genuine concern.

'I'm fine,' I said, trying to sound convincing, 'just a bit of a headache. Nothing that two aspirin and a good night out can't fix.' I winked at her with a devilish grin to hide my discomfort.

'Oh, yes,' she replied, slipping on her dress. 'This party is going to be amazing! And I have already seen that Gaurav will not be attending, so you and I are free to be ourselves the whole night.' I leaned forward to help zip her dress up. She stepped back, motioning for me to examine her.

'I have the perfect jacket to go with that.' I hopped off my bed and took out a black high-necked biker jacket. I searched through my costume jewellery and gave her a pair of light blue drop earrings and some matching stack bracelets, telling her to wear the boots instead of the pumps. When she was done, I changed into my outfit for the evening—a full-length gold jumpsuit with a low-cut V-neck and a cut-out back. I wore my high gold wedges and kept my jewellery to a minimum, only wearing a black cuff bracelet that would match my black clutch.

'Oh my god, Jhanvi, you look amazing!' Latika said as I came back into the bedroom. The energy drink and vodka were beginning to work, and I felt my energy levels begin to rise.

'Would you take a picture of me?' I asked as I handed her my phone. 'I'll return the favour.' I posed and posted the first photo of the evening, making sure that the promoter and the club were tagged. This was a huge deal and would lead to bigger sponsorship and brand deals.

'No, no. Turn your arm inward,' I directed Latika while I took her photos. 'Like this, see?' I showed her how her arm should be placed to give the illusion of length and slimness. 'Look here,' I swiped between two photos that showed her pose versus mine. She looked at me, shocked.

'That's a massive difference!'

'I know,' I told her. 'I'll help you tonight, maybe we can get you some new followers.' My phone rang; the car was waiting for us downstairs. I couldn't help comparing her to Kavya. This life wasn't new to Latika; she knew the drill; it wasn't exciting.

'The car is waiting for us.' I downed my drink before picking up my clutch. Latika followed suit.

In the car to the club, we chatted briefly, but I couldn't speak much, I needed to monitor my stats and go through the evening's itinerary. Latika seemed content, chatting to her boyfriend and scrolling through her social media.

When we reached the club, we saw hundreds of people standing around, waiting to enter. The music from inside was loud—we had been able to hear it when turning into the street. We got out of the cab and were greeted by the club owner. He extended his hand and leaned closer so that I could hear him over the noise of the crowds, who were anxious to get into the club and start their evening.

'So, you will cut the ribbon and then we will escort you in.' I nodded in acknowledgement, feeling overwhelmed. 'Once inside, you will do a thirty-minute meet and greet in the VIP area with our competition winners, and then the rest of the evening is yours.'

'Thanks,' I muttered, trying to smile through the anxiety I could feel building inside me. I felt out of my depth, like I didn't belong. This was something I had wanted for so long, and now that I had it, I wasn't sure if it really was everything it was cut out to be. I forced the thoughts out of my head, trying to focus on the task at hand. Cut the ribbon, take some photos and then the rest of the night was mine.

The ceremonial scissors felt heavy in my hand, as I cut the ribbon to the cheers of the party-goers who were blocked off by a velvet rope. Inside, I was handed a glass of champagne and shown to the VIP area. The sweet bubbles burned my throat and stomach, but soon, the familiar warmth took over.

'I love you!' A girl entered the VIP area, clutching her phone, which was already open on my social media profile.

'Thank you,' I said, posing for a selfie with her. 'So, what do you do?' Small talk was going to be tedious for the next few minutes, but I knew that it was the price I needed to pay for an all-expenses-paid evening. Between chatting with the competition winners, I eagerly sipped my champagne, willing the nerves to leave me, trying desperately to calm my mind. I could no longer tell whether I was tired or not. The constant need to be online meant that I was awake more hours than I was asleep. Perhaps that was what was bringing on the feeling of dread inside me.

'Could I have a double vodka and whatever energy drink you have please,' I asked the waiter who was hovering near us. He nodded, and not long after drinking it, I began to feel better; I could feel my anxiety leaving me.

'Are you done?' Latika flopped herself down on the couch to take a selfie.

'I think so,' I answered.

'Then let's have a party!' she yelled, pulling me from the couch towards the dance floor. She handed me two shots as I joined the throngs of people moving to the rhythm of the electronic music playing. This week had been tough—no Kavya and a true sense of loneliness. While I had said I wanted to be alone, I hadn't known what it meant. Without Kavya, this seemed pointless.

Lost in my thoughts, I allowed the music to take control of my body as I swayed to the primal sounds of the bass. With one shot after another, I dispelled the thoughts inside me; those feelings of emptiness, of being lost. My body was frail from the lack of nutrition since Kavya had stopped coming around with food. From Monday, I would begin to take care of myself, I told myself. Eat better and drink less. But, for now. Tonight. I wanted to forget that my life wasn't as perfect as I expected it to be.

Behind me, Latika danced enthusiastically with the crowd, but I was content to be alone. The same way I had been as a child. Present, but not participating. The more my body resisted my drive to see the evening out, the more determined I was to push through it. Not caring anymore about my perfect image, I danced. I danced away my pain, danced away the loneliness and the pressure to appear perfect. A hand on my arm pulled me from my trance as Latika leaned over.

'Are you okay?' Latika shouted into my ear.

'Fine,' I shouted back, holding her hand.

'Jhanvi, you don't look well.' She had genuine concern in her eyes. I pushed her away from me, expecting her to lecture me about my drinking in the same way that Kavya had. Lovingly, she took my hand, and led me to the bathroom.

'You look sick,' she said, as the doors closed behind us. 'Is your head still sore?'

I nodded, not wanting to acknowledge that I felt nauseous from the alcohol and lack of food.

'Here.' She wet her hand under the cold water tap and patted the back of my neck. Waves of nausea overtook me as I leaned over the basin, my body ridding itself of the toxicity I had spent the last five days pumping into it. The bathroom door opened, and laughter and music filled the room.

'Is she puking?' An unfamiliar voice broke the sounds of me emptying my stomach.

'Get lost,' Latika shouted. A flash from what I was sure was a camera broke the dimly lit bathroom.

'Hey!' Latika seemed to be shouting at the girl. I couldn't move. Glued to the cold basin, I couldn't let go. The room spun too viciously, and I wasn't sure that I was done throwing up. Back at my side, Latika moved my hair out of my face.

'We need to go, have you got your bag?' I shook my head; it was still on the couch in the VIP area.

'I'll get it, stay here,' I nodded my head, unable to speak.

It felt like an eternity, but when she got back, I was standing against the basin. I washed all of the mess away and made sure to straighten myself up. We left the club quickly, without telling the hosts, which I knew would negatively affect my relationship with them, but Latika was right. I needed to get out, and quickly.

Back home, Latika helped me into my bed and insisted she would stay the night. I resisted, telling her it was just something I ate. I was fine. When she closed the door behind her, I opened my phone. There was a message from Kavya, which I decided to deal with the next day, when I was sober. I posted a photo from the club to my timeline, hashtagged it as best I could, and sent a message to the promoter explaining that I was sick, and I thought it best to leave. And that they shouldn't listen to rumours floating around about my behaviour.

I was exhausted, but the energy drinks were still flowing through my body. Standing up, I went to my closet and began planning the following week's outfits.

Perfection, the art of striving to have no flaws; it was what society expected of us, and it is the unreal life portrayed in every publication, on every billboard, on every social media account. Anything less than perfection could not be accepted in this world; my world. I sat down on the floor and closed my eyes. I thought tears would come, but they didn't, they couldn't, because perfection demanded that they stay buried deep inside of me. Sleep was fitful and barely worth the effort. Walking through to the bathroom, I turned the light on and looked at myself in the mirror. My life was perfect, I told myself determinedly.

22

ASHRAY

Life is fluid, ever-changing; a fleeting moment, as Maa used to say. Everyone who enters your life must leave it eventually. How you choose to spend your time with them is entirely up to you. These were the words she used to say to me when my feelings of abandonment bubbled to the surface. Her words pulled me out of the darkest times of my life. Perhaps that was why I insisted on loving everyone that I allowed to enter my life. Part of me always knew the day would come when they would leave; but not so soon, not this way.

'Ashray, come and sit with us a little bit,' Maa called me from the kitchen into the living room. I was reading about my newest prospective client, formulating a plan. Laughter filled our little apartment. Part of me didn't want to give this up. Our apartment was cosy, it was my childhood home, but Maa needed this, and I needed it to prove to myself that I was better than what Sakshi had done to me.

'Coming,' I shouted from the kitchen. Rishi's words were inaudible, but Maa's laughter was heart-warming.

'What is this clown saying that is so funny?' I said as I walked into the living room. The two looked at me guiltily before laughing again.

'Rishi was telling me about your first flight,' she told me. 'My boy, you have always been so nervous about taking a step forward, but when you do, you fly.' She almost swallowed the last word, realising too late what she had said. Rishi bent over laughing, and I couldn't help but join them. I sat on the couch next to Maa, patting her hand as we composed ourselves.

'So, tell me more about your plans for the apartment,' I said to Maa as she wiped away a joyful tear.

'I cannot wait to plant some chillies in the pots outside,' she said. 'Do you think that we can put a table and chairs out on the main balcony?' I nodded, knowing that she was thinking about having dinners like this outside.

Rishi was on his phone typing a message, but my Maa didn't seem to mind.

'Your girlfriend?' I asked as he put his phone in his pocket.

'Yes, and my mom and dad. Being here makes me miss them a little.'

I'd forgotten that they were in Mexico. 'It must be difficult,' I said to him.

'I do miss them, but when I need them, we video call, and we phone each other at least three times a week.' I loved that Rishi was still so connected to his parents, but I suspected that he was making light of how much he missed having them in his daily life.

'How about some tea?' My Maa stood up from her chair. I stood to help her, but she put her hand on my shoulder, urging me to sit again.

'Sit, Ashray. Speak with Rishi a little bit. Maybe you can sign those papers for the apartment.' I looked over at him, and he nodded.

'Go and fetch your laptop, and we will sign them digitally,' he said.

I rose to fetch my laptop from the kitchen, taking out three cups while I was in there. Maa patted me on the cheek as I walked out and I kissed her gently on the forehead. 'I love you, Maa.' She smiled as she walked past me into the kitchen.

'I love you, son,' she said quietly, as she put the kettle on for our tea.

In the living room, I opened the email Rishi had sent me from his mobile and read through the lease document. I opened the sign document tab, took a deep breath and digitally signed the lease for our new apartment. Rishi patted me on the back.

'Welcome to your new life, Ashray,' he said, grinning. I smiled back, truly happy at the decision I had made. From the kitchen, the kettle started to whistle. I closed my laptop and placed it on the coffee table; I would put it away later. The kettle got louder. Maa zoned into her newspaper adverts often, but the sound was beginning to push through to the living room. I glanced towards the kitchen.

'Do you want to go and check?' Rishi asked me. I shook my head, knowing that Maa would be irritated if I interrupted her routine.

'I think you should,' Rishi said, 'maybe the button is stuck?'

'Maa?' I called out as I stuck my head into the kitchen, not wanting to frighten her, knowing she would be buried in her newspaper. The kettle steamed on the stove, but my Maa wasn't there. I turned the stove off and poured the hot water into the teapot so the tea could brew. I turned towards the corridor, shouting that the tea was already in the pot, before turning back to the living room. To this day, I cannot tell you what made me turn back to look down the corridor again, or why I didn't see it the first time. I have played the situation over in my head so many times; agonised, analysed and beaten myself up over it. But it doesn't matter why I did, only that when I did turn back, I saw her foot.

'Maa?' I called down the corridor, trying not to panic, but my legs betrayed me. She was lying face down in the bathroom, and instinct told me to roll her over. Her body felt so frail as I gently placed her on her back. I realised how cold the tiled floor was.

'Rishi! Call an ambulance!' I couldn't hide the panic in my voice, trying to remember the basic first aid course we attended in college. Rishi appeared behind me, reaching into his pocket for his phone. I could see his concern.

'Maa, please,' I begged her, while I tried to find a pulse in her neck as we had been taught. I heard Rishi give the paramedics our address, as I ran my fingers down her breastbone, trying desperately to rack my brain, worrying that I may hurt the woman who gave me my life.

'One, two, three,' I began to count the times that I pressed down on her chest, willing her heart to begin beating again. Listening to her chest, there was nothing. I thought back to weeks earlier, when I had cried about Sakshi abandoning me. It all seemed so irrelevant now. Back then, the sound of her heart beating had comforted me. Now, her chest seemed empty. I breathed deeply into her mouth and began pushing on her chest again.

'How long are they going to be?' I shouted at Rishi. I didn't want this responsibility.

'Five minutes, Ashray.' Rishi was pacing like a madman, waiting to open the door for the paramedics as soon as they arrived.

'Maa,' I leaned over, listening for her heart through my own sobbing. I breathed air into her lungs again. 'Please.' I counted out loud, praying to any deity that would hear my pleas to bring her back.

'Good job, you can step back now.' Through my tears, I saw three paramedics. One of them tried to pull me off her chest, but my body seemed to be acting separately from what my rational brain was telling me. Then another set of hands were on me; this time they were familiar.

'Ashray, let them work,' Rishi said gently. I stood up and stepped out of the way. Rishi led me into the living room. The voices from down the passage seemed garbled, I couldn't make out what they were saying. The room felt like it was spinning, closing in. Another set of paramedics entered the apartment with a stretcher. I put my head in my hands, convincing myself that they wouldn't take a deceased person out on a stretcher.

'How will they get her down the stairs?' I asked Rishi.

'They know how to do these things, Ashray. Let's just let them do what they do best.' A woman in uniform kneeled down in front of me.

'I need to ask you a few questions,' she began. She was so compassionate, I couldn't help but think of Sakshi and her training.

'What is her name?'

'Akshita,' I said, not wanting to make eye contact with her. Worried that by somehow locking eyes with the woman who was trying to save my Maa, I would be told a truth I wasn't ready for.

'Is she your mother?'

I nodded.

'Your name?'

'Ashray.'

'Ashray, we can't be certain, but it looks like your mother has had a heart attack. We have got her back, but I need you to understand that—' I didn't allow her to finish.

'She's alive?'

'Technically, yes, but Ashray ...' Nothing else she said was important. My Maa was alive. Her heart was beating again, everything else I could deal with.

'We will take her to the hospital by ambulance. Will you both come with us to the hospital?'

Rishi shook his head.

'I will stay here and clean up.' He looked at me. 'I will take a bus there when I'm done.' I was grateful that my friend wanted to spare me from the mess he knew would be left behind. They wheeled her past me, a bag valve mask on her to help her breathe.

In the ambulance, she squeezed my hand lightly; I was sure of it. I put her hand to my cheek. 'Life is fleeting, it is temporary, and it should be spent loving the people you choose to let into your life. Everyone who enters your life must leave it eventually. How you choose to spend your time with them is entirely up to you.' I repeated those words over and over again on the way to the hospital. Willing our fleeting moment to be extended.

23
JHANVI

'You're a beautiful girl, Jhanvi …' Why was I thinking about my mom? 'But you need to look after yourself. There is going to come a time when Dad and I can't be there to beg you to eat.' What the hell was wrong with me? I pulled my attention back to my screen, willing my eyes to focus on what was happening to my account. For the first time since I had got on social media, my numbers were decreasing. Perhaps it was a glitch. I had heard of followers being deleted for no reason, and a quick email sorted the issue out. But I couldn't focus. My body fought my brain that begged for some sleep.

'Oh, for goodness sake!' I stood up in frustration after dropping my phone for the umpteenth time. Somewhere in this mess was another box of dieting tablets, I knew that. Frantically, I searched under piles of clothes for the clear blister pack. I wanted to cry, to scream. Why could I never find things when I needed them? I picked up a bag of makeup and emptied it out onto the rug. The pink pills stared back at me. I grabbed the pack and marched through to the kitchen.

'You need to look after yourself,' my mom's words continued to echo in my mind.

'Shut up!' I screamed, as I pushed four tablets out onto the kitchen counter, frantic to stay awake and fix whatever was happening with my online life. I grabbed the bottle of vodka on the counter and swallowed the pills. Ignoring my body's reaction to the alcohol, I grabbed an energy drink out of my fridge. Back in the living room, I retrieved my phone from where it lay on the floor and sat on the couch. I had lost twenty thousand followers overnight. Why? Nothing was untoward—I had posted as I usually had. I checked every detail, down to the spelling of my hashtags, trying to figure it out. Finally, I convinced myself that it was a system error. It had to be! I typed an email asking the powers that be what had happened to my followers. Unlike other influencers, I didn't buy my followers, there were no fake accounts on my profile.

I opened my messages to respond to Kavya, hoping that we could reconcile, wanting desperately to have her back in my life. Six messages from her. I held my breath, expecting a tirade of angry words from her. I deserved it after what I'd said to her.

'Sure.'

'Are you okay?'

'Jhanvi?'

'I see you are at a club opening.'

'Jhanvi! Are you okay?'

The last one was sent ten minutes ago.

'I saw what happened at the club on social media?'

What the hell did she mean? What happened at the club? My stomach rolled in the same way that it would if I was at sea. The bathroom. Those girls. The flash.

'No! No! No!' I shot up from my couch. They had taken a photo and posted it to social media. Quickly, I opened my account; my numbers had fallen further.

'No!' I screamed into my empty apartment. 'How dare they!' My heart was pounding. I knew this feeling; it was panic and anger—the same feelings that Gaurav and Puneet had stirred up with their infidelity.

I paced about as the room began to spin. My apartment was littered with remnants of how I had been neglecting myself, but I forced myself to look beyond it. 'Not now,' I told myself as my stomach protested. Blackness crept in from my peripheral vision. It was so subtle that I didn't have the time to react to what was happening. My body betrayed me, my eyes no longer seeing. The last thing I remember was cursing, wondering if I would wake up this time and, if I didn't, how long it would take for someone to find me.

The scientific term is hypnagogic: the state between being awake and asleep. When the conscious mind fights the brain to return to the land of the living, somewhere between hallucination and paralysis as the body begins to function once more. For me, it felt never-ending. A blow by blow of everything I had done wrong in life, everything that made me imperfect.

'Wake up. What did you take?'

How fitting that the girl who grew up surrounded by so many people should leave this world in the same way.

'I don't know. I just got here, and she was like this.'

I fought so hard to leave home. To avoid marriage and to not become another statistic, and now, that is what my life was. I was a statistic, a girl behind a screen, and I couldn't escape it. Didn't know how to be anyone other than the person I taught myself to be.

'It's beating, but it's fast. Too fast! Hurry, please!'

Would they miss me? The countless faces who couldn't wait to pull back the curtain several times a day to look into my life. Voyeurs; that was what humanity had become. A sick, twisted game of watching while others strived for perfection and berating ourselves for never reaching those levels. I was one of them. Peeping into other's lives, pushing myself to be everything that I saw at their show.

'Can you move aside? We need to work on her.'

And what of those few who actually knew me. What would they say about what I have become? A mess on the floor amongst all the things society threw at me to sell. An object, to be sold with other objects.

'*We're taking her into Lifeline. Are you going to ride along?*'

I promised to phone Mom first this weekend. Would she think I had forgotten again? Or, knowing that a lot of the time I avoided our strained conversations, decided not to call? Her voice still echoed in my mind; my imagination allowed me to think about her agony over my self-neglect. She cared. I knew she did. Why could she never show me, though?

'*What is wrong with her?*'

A question I have been asking myself for so long. What is wrong with me? All of this hard work, all of this pain, and I self-destruct, exactly as I always have. Two words. That's all it would have taken for me not to be laying here, unaware of whether I was alive or dead.

'*We have given her something to slow her heart rate down.*'

Two words I have never been able to say.

Help. Me.

Everything has a breaking point. A point where the external pressure placed on an object becomes too much for it to bear and it snaps, shatters, breaks. The thing about a breaking point is there is always an option to turn back, to stop adding the pressure that will cause the object to break. To yield the relentless push and pull and let go, release and allow it to just be.

I opened my eyes. Sunlight flooded through a window in a room that was not my own. Panic rose as I remembered the morning at the Goa Music Festival, when I awoke in a tent, not knowing where I was or what had happened to me. I tried to move, but my body refused, completely unwilling to listen to my command. I blinked and looked up at the white ceiling. My body ached, and my skin itched. My hand on my stomach told me that what I was wearing did not belong to me. I didn't try to talk, there was no point; I was alone, I knew that. I was always alone. Finally, my body responded, if only out of pure instinct from the dull pain in my lower back. I rolled towards the window, hoping that some sun would help to orient me a little. Pain seared up my hand as I met resistance mid-roll. A drip. I was in a hospital. Someone had found me.

I closed my eyes, wanting to sleep again. A familiar hand took mine. I felt the warmth and the softness, the touch I craved so much. The hands felt older, but they were still her hands, my mom's skin against mine. My mind fought my body, reminding me that my mom was more than a thousand kilometres away, but it felt real. She felt real.

'Jhanvi?' Her voice pulled me out of my agonising internal battle.

'Mom?' My voice no longer sounded like mine. It was hoarse, and I couldn't seem to find any strength to say what I wanted to say.

'How are you feeling?'

I rolled over to see her concerned eyes searching my face. I thought it looked like she had been crying.

'I'm fine, Mom.' I tried to sit up in the hospital bed, but the room began spinning again. I leaned back, willing my body to respond to what I wanted it to do. I was far from fine.

'Kavya found you,' she said, holding on to my hand tightly. 'You were on the floor in your apartment.' I nodded my head, knowing that a lecture was coming.

'How did she get in?'

My mother shrugged. That detail was unimportant to her. 'Dad is here, speaking to the doctor downstairs. Jhanvi, you could have died.' She stifled a sob.

My dad entered the room then, and a doctor followed him in. Their words sounded jumbled: my liver was suffering, my body shutting down. I was thin, too thin, and dehydration was affecting my kidneys. All I heard was that I had failed, once more at the simplest of things, at something I was born with. Beauty.

'You need to take care of yourself now.' My father's voice pulled me from my thoughts. 'This is serious, Jhanvi. Next time you could die.' I wanted to cry, not because of my own mortality, but because I felt humiliated. Like I was a failure.

'Where's Kavya?' I asked my mom, wanting to see her, needing to apologise for everything I had said to her.

My father perched himself on the side of my bed. 'She's downstairs, she hasn't left since you were admitted.'

'We had a fight, I said horrible things to her. Why would she come to my apartment? Why would she save me?' My mother gasped at my words, not wanting to believe what was coming out of my mouth. Tears welled in my father's eyes.

'Because we all love you, Jhanvi,' my dad's voice broke the silence in the room. 'Is it so difficult to believe that there are people who would be devastated if you were no longer ...' He couldn't say the last words. I turned my head away from him, not wanting to see the pain I was inflicting on my parents, knowing that they had dropped everything to get here.

I saw Kavya coming down the corridor, although I didn't need to physically see her. I felt her presence in the same way that I did when I collapsed. Kavya was tired, and I could see she had been crying.

'May I come in?' She looked at my parents, asking their permission to see me but also apologising for intruding on what she thought was a private moment between us. My mom nodded, smiling slightly.

'Maybe you can talk some sense into her,' she said.

'Doubtful,' Kavya said and smiled down at me. 'But I will try.' She sat down on my bed and ran her fingers through my hair, the way she always did when I felt down.

'Jhanvi, you have to stop this. I thought you were dead. You and I have so much we still need to do. So many dreams. You have to talk to someone. It doesn't have to be us, but it needs to be someone. Please.' I couldn't answer her, I didn't know how to open up. My mom stood up, sensing that I needed privacy to say everything that was pressing so heavily on my heart. My dad followed suit and the two of them left the room. I looked at Kavya, wanting her to understand that the words I was going to say to her were sincere, not another attempt at avoiding an argument with her.

'I'm sorry,' I said as I reached for her hand, 'for everything. For the way I treated you, what I said, for lying to you. I just ...'

She shook her head, not wanting to hear anything more. I knew she had forgiven me long before I blacked out, before I even messaged her, asking to talk; but I needed to say the words.

'Kavya, I can think of a million reasons why I should not be an influencer, a million reasons why this life isn't for me, and they all revolve around what I could do better. How I could possibly be better. But none of them is you. You keep me grounded, and as stubborn as I am, you always push back.'

'I know,' she said, 'but you can still do this healthily, Jhanvi. Show people, young girls, that perfection lies in the imperfect.'

'I am sorry to interrupt, but she needs her rest, and visiting hours are over.' A young nurse stood at my door, warmth radiating from her smile. Kavya nodded before kissing my head.

'I'm going to go home and shower. I'll be back tonight, okay?'

I nodded and managed a smile. They left the room, the nurse closing the door behind her. Kavya was right, I could come back from this in a healthy way; I could prove those girls in the bathroom wrong.

I saw that my phone was on the cabinet next to my bed. I started it up and took a photo of the IV in my hand, making sure to have the hospital bed in the background. I uploaded the photo to my social media.

#notdrunk #actuallysick #hospital #dontbelievelies

I hit the post button.

24
ASHRAY

There are moments in our lives that change us irrevocably; these moments come without warning. Sometimes they are avoidable. Other times, it is a cruel throw of the dice.

Walking behind the paramedics into the hospital, time didn't speed up. Every movement the doctors made seemed to last a lifetime. Closing the curtain around her bed, they shielded me from what they were doing to her, and it seemed to take an eternity. But she was alive, and that's what mattered. Nothing further had happened in the ambulance trip to Lifeline; she was stable, and that was a good sign, even if she wasn't breathing on her own yet.

'Ashray?' A voice I didn't want to hear brought me back to the present. Sakshi stood in front of me in a nurse's uniform.

'Serendipity,' I thought.

'You need to move to the waiting room until we have some news for you.'

I allowed her to lead me to the small lounge, not wanting to say anything, not prepared to speak to her at all. Rishi walked in with an overnight bag and rolled his eyes when he saw Sakshi.

'I packed you a bag. Didn't know if I should bring anything for your Maa.'

'They have her in the Emergency Room,' I said. 'She's alive though. She's not breathing by herself, but she's alive.' I needed some reassuring words from him.

'I'm so sorry, Ashray,' Sakshi said, standing at the door.

'I think you should leave,' Rishi said; he did not want me to have to deal with any more pressure. He wanted to take away the additional discomfort.

'What happened, Rishi?' I asked, still confused by what had happened at our apartment. 'One minute we were laughing and planning our future and the next, this.'

'We can't always plan the future, Ashray, sometimes things just happen.'

'I was supposed to take her to the doctor weeks ago, and I didn't.' I stifled a sob.

'Ashray, this isn't your fault. None of this is. Come on, hey, it's going to be fine.' He didn't sound very convincing.

'Ashray?' A doctor walked into the waiting room, a file in his hand. I stood to greet him. 'I'm Dr Patel. Your mother has had a massive cardiac event, but she is fighting. We have her on a respirator to take some pressure off her heart, but she is going to need surgery.' The colour drained from my face. 'These forms need to be signed, giving us permission to take her in for the bypass surgery she needs.' I reached out to take the pen, hesitating for a moment.

'What will happen if she doesn't have the surgery?' I asked.

'Ashray, your mother is very sick. Without the surgery, she most likely won't make it. The surgery is risky, but at least you're giving her a chance.' I didn't want to make the decision; the pressure was too much. Why did I have to make the decision to allow my mother to live or die?

I signed the papers. 'Do the surgery, bring her back to me, please.' The doctor shook my hand and left the room.

'You might as well go home,' I said to Rishi. 'There is no point in neither of us being at work tomorrow.'

Rishi nodded. 'I'll tell Vihaan what happened,' he said, giving me a hug and patting me on my back.

In the room alone, scenarios played over and over in my head. I would need to make sure everything was moved to the new apartment before Maa was discharged. I didn't even know how long recovery for this kind of surgery took, but I knew that when she was discharged from the hospital, getting her up a flight of stairs would be impossible. I looked at the clock, two hours had passed since we had left home in the back of an ambulance. I opened the overnight bag Rishi had packed; he knew me so well already. I took out my laptop and switched it on to distract myself from watching the clock. The portfolio was almost done when a nurse popped in, asking me if I would like a cup of coffee.

I nodded and then asked, 'How long do these kind of things take?'

'It depends,' she said. 'If it is a complicated case with a large amount of damage, it can take hours.'

'Do you know anything about how the surgery is going?'

'No,' she said, adding, 'One of the doctors will come see you if there is any news.'

I looked at the clock; three-and-a-half hours. Clicking the multi-coloured circle on my screen, the internet browser opened up. I wanted to see what would be needed for Maa's recovery. Articles popped up, and I took down details. The prognosis seemed good, and I allowed myself to relax a little. I closed my eyes, allowing sleep to take hold of me.

A knock on the door startled me awake. I sat up, disorientated. The doctor who had come by earlier walked into the waiting room, urging me to remain seated. He sat next to me, no files in his hand this time.

'The damage to your mother's heart was extensive,' he began. 'When we opened her chest up, it became apparent exactly how bad the initial heart attack was.' What was he trying to tell me?

'Her heart was beating when she went in for surgery ...'

'She had severe tachycardia, Ashray.'

'What is that?' I asked.

'It's when the heart starts beating again at a rate that is too fast.' He paused for a moment. 'A heart that has tachycardia after a massive cardiac event cannot be repaired.'

'I don't understand.' I stood up, unable to control my reaction to what was happening.

'We tried, really we did, but we couldn't bring her back.'

'No!' I shouted. 'No! No! No! She was alive when she came in here. She was alive! Her heart was beating!' The walls began to close in.

'I know, but there was nothing we could do, Ashray. It wasn't going to last long. I'm so sorry for your loss.'

Pain radiated down my arms, and I couldn't breathe. My heart was beating so fast, I thought it would burst out of my chest. I could hear the blood rushing in my ears.

'Are you all right?' the doctor said, putting his hand on my shoulder. Gone. She was gone. I wouldn't bring her home; she would never cook in our new kitchen; and she would never see the Mumbai view from our balcony while we ate dinner together.

'Are you all right?' he asked again. I couldn't breathe, wanting desperately to join my Maa in the afterlife. My stomach twisted in a knot, nausea and pressure driving my panic.

'Nurse! Nurse!' he called out, and Sakshi ran into the room. Perfect, just perfect!

'Ashray, breathe,' she said, trying to get me to calm down. 'You're having a panic attack, Ashray. Please breathe.' I fell to my knees, the room closing in on me.

'Bring me Ativan,' I heard the doctor shout through the pounding in my ears. A needle entered my skin and the drug coursed through my body slowly, bringing my heart rate down to a regular pace. My breathing slowed, although the pressure was still there, and my chest burned.

'Ashray, you need to control your breathing, or you're going to have another panic attack,' Sakshi said, hovering over me.

'I just need you to leave the room,' I shouted. I wanted her out of my life. Out of the most traumatic thing that had ever happened to me. She had no place here. She left the room quickly, and another nurse entered. The doctor shone a light into my eyes, checking for something, I wasn't sure what.

'Get this man a bed,' he barked to someone outside the waiting room. 'Nurse, let's get his breathing under control.' The nurse kneeled in front of me.

'Look at me,' she said, and put her hand on my chin, guiding my eyes to hers. 'Breathe in and out with me, okay?' I nodded. She was an older woman, and her eyes implored me to try and control what was happening. 'Deep breath in and out, again,' she said. I mimicked her breathing. I had no control over what happened next, no control over my body or my mind. She looked like she understood, looked like she would understand. I leaned forward, my head on her chest— her heartbeat drowning out the blood rushing in my ears—and I cried. A sound that shouldn't have come from me; a howl that could only be described as animalistic pain.

'Why?' The word escaped my mouth. She put her hand on my head and hushed me. Down the passage, a bed was pushed quickly. They lifted me off the floor onto the bed, crying, battling to breathe, fighting my own racing heart.

Why?

25

JHANVI

'You can go home today.' The nurse hovered over me, listening to my heartbeat. I couldn't shake the feeling that I knew her from somewhere. 'You need to make sure that you eat well, okay?' Everyone was going on about my weight; but that wasn't the problem. The problem was the damage that was done to my reputation because of two wannabes in a bathroom.

'I will,' I said and smiled sweetly at her. Kavya had dropped off my keys the day before, telling me that she had not left back her set after our fight. My mom helped me into my clothes. My body was sore, but only because I'd been forced to lay in bed for so long. Thankfully, I had plenty of material that I could post, and my stats seemed to be recovering since my first honest piece of content, about me being in a hospital. Some people had alluded to me being in rehab, which I rubbished immediately.

'This is the number of one of our psychiatrists. He is really good. We suggest that you see him to get yourself back on track.' I nodded, although I didn't feel like there was anything major wrong with me to warrant seeing a psychiatrist.

'When we get back to your apartment, we'll talk,' my mom said, trying to start the conversation I didn't want to have.

'Mom, I'm fine, really. I've learned from what happened, and I will make sure it never happens again.' My dad patted my mom on the back, which I knew meant that the conversation was only being stalled until later. Suddenly, staying in the hospital seemed like a better idea. Kavya saved me from my impending misery.

'Look what I brought you,' she said, breezing into my hospital room, a small light pink bag in her hand. I opened it excitedly. Inside were my Nike sneakers, some makeup and a pair of oversized glasses.

'You're amazing.' I reached out to hug her, and she laughed as she embraced me. My friend was back in my life, and I was so grateful to her for forgiving me. Without Kavya, I wasn't sure I would have made it back from this. The taxi ride home was awkward. My mom wouldn't give me my phone and, I have to admit, I pouted in exactly the same way I used to when I was a child. Slipping the key into my door, we walked into my apartment. I groaned; pill packets and vodka bottles littered my living room, the smell from the now rotting fruits permeated the musty two-bedroom apartment I called home.

'What is this?' My mom was the first to speak. Kavya mouthed that she was sorry. I knew that she hadn't had the time to clean up my mess, but part of me thought that perhaps she had left it this way to show them how out of control I was.

'I was busy, Mom,' I whined, trying to use every tactic I used to when I was a teenager. It didn't work.

'Jhanvi, this is unacceptable.' I felt like I was seven again. My dad shook his head at me, unable to hide his disappointment.

'How did it get this bad?' he asked me. I shrugged, not knowing what to say.

'You will come to Delhi with us, this cannot be allowed to continue.' I looked up at him, mouth open.

'Dad, no! You two cannot come into my home and start dictating to me how to live my life!' I didn't know why I was suddenly comfortable letting them know how I felt. 'I'm an adult, and you have absolutely no authority over what I do or do not do anymore.'

'I'll be in the kitchen,' Kavya said, trying to escape the tension that was mounting.

My mom sat down on the couch, pushing aside a pile of clothes. I sat on the opposite side of the room, scanning the area where my body had lain fighting to survive a few days earlier.

'There are good doctors in Delhi, Jhanvi, doctors who can fix this,' my mom said, trying to reassure me that they weren't attacking me. But, as always, it felt like a personal attack.

'Fix what, Mom? Me? I'm not broken. I was busy. Distracted. I made a mistake, and I will rectify it.' I tried to hide my hurt at what was said.

'We are not saying you are broken, Jhanvi, but something is wrong. This,' she threw her arms around, wildly gesturing at the room, 'this is not normal! You need help!'

'You don't get it! You never have, because you don't listen to me.'

'We always listen to you,' my dad interjected, hurt by my words.

'No, Dad, you don't. You come here after finding out that I almost died, and your solution is to tell me that I am broken and I need to come back to Delhi to be fixed.' I was met by their gazes on either side of me, not knowing if what I said caused them pain or if they were angry at me for finally saying what was on my mind. Either way, I was tired and needed to get my life back. There were commitments to be met, and I was sure that although my sponsors would understand to begin with, soon they would find someone to replace me. 'This is pointless,' I said, reaching for my phone.

'Jhanvi, put that thing down. We need to talk,' my dad said sternly. His tone warned me not to challenge him.

'Or what, Dad? You'll have me committed a thousand kilometres away? Shoved in a room and put on medication while a panel of doctors tries to figure out why my mind is broken? I'm sure that will do wonders for your reputation.' I rolled my eyes. My mom reached out and took my phone from my hand.

'Jhanvi, we really do need to talk.' I looked up, ready to fight. I felt like I was being caged in, reminded of my imperfections.

'All anyone does in this family is talk, nobody ever listens,' I said calmly.

'We're listening now,' she said, genuine concern on her face. For a moment, I contemplated not saying anything, telling them to leave and allowing them time to cool down, but my mom was right. We did need to talk, and it was my turn.

'My whole life I have been expected to be perfect.'

'Jhanvi, that isn't true,' my dad interrupted.

'But it is, Dad. Hide my emotions, don't cry in public, no physical touching when there were friends around, and you always had friends around. I was your damned accessory. Your pretty, perfect doll that you could put away when everyone went home. You never loved me! Never showed me you loved me, and it hurt, every damned day of my life. You want to know why I need to be perfect all the time? It's because you programmed me that way. Because if I was perfect, if I did just one thing right in your eyes, then maybe, just maybe, you would love me. But I had to almost die for Mom to even hold my hand, and you still haven't touched me, have you, Dad?' His brows furrowed deeply, my words once again causing pain. Why did I do this? Why couldn't I just go back to the days of turning a blind eye? Back to before Puneet.

My dad lifted himself off the couch and kneeled down at my feet. 'My sweet child, you think we don't love you? That I don't love you?' I nodded my head, stubborn in my conviction. 'Jhanvi. The day you were born is still the best day of my life, and every milestone, every success, we are behind you, telling everyone how proud we are of you. I was raised in a different time, Jhanvi, in a time when you didn't show love through physical affection. For me, love was always about praise. If I knew,' his voice choked, 'if I knew that all you needed was for me to reach out and hold you once in a while, I would have done it.'

I began to cry, finally hearing the words I had longed for my whole life. 'We tell you that you are perfect, Jhanvi, because to us you are.' He wrapped his arms around my neck, pulling me into him. I sobbed. Feeling my father's arms around me, I knew that what he said was the truth. 'So, come to Delhi, and we can fix this?' he asked.

'No, Dad, I need to sort this out by myself.'

'How about I move in?' Kavya stood in the kitchen doorway, yellow plastic gloves covering her hands. She had been cleaning my kitchen again; and like a madwoman, I felt like laughing. 'I can make sure that Jhanvi gets back on track with her diet and I enjoy helping her with her work. It really is very interesting. What do you say, Jhanvi? Do you have an opening for an executive assistant?' I smiled; my best friend to the rescue again.

My mom shook her head, not convinced that it was enough.

'I'll see the psychiatrist that the nurse recommended. Kavya can drop me for every appointment and make sure I go in. I don't want to go back to Delhi, please,' I begged. 'This is my home. I know it doesn't look like much, but I like my life. I just ...' remembering the moment I lay motionless on this very floor, I looked my mom in the eyes and said, '... I need help.' Visibly, my mom relaxed, in the same way that I had moments earlier in my dad's embrace. She could relax because I knew it now. I knew I needed help.

'Okay, if that's what you want, then we will do it your way, but I'll stay back with you for a few more days. And Jhanvi, we want to hear from you more than once a week. Okay?' my mom said. 'And video call your parents once in a while. I know it's hard for you to understand, but we miss you terribly.' She stood up from the couch, arms open, welcoming me into a hug.

The rest of the evening was spent cleaning up my apartment and laughing. By the time my dad was ready to leave, I felt that I had some semblance of control again. My mom had her arm around me as my dad left my apartment, promising to phone me as soon as he landed in Delhi. I hugged him and closed the door.

'So, I'll sleep at my place tonight,' Kavya said. 'And then, tomorrow, I will bring some of my things over. Until Aunty goes back to Delhi, I will sleep in your bed. It will be like a teenage sleepover,' she said with a grin. I smiled, but I knew I wasn't very convincing. My mom was unpacking her things in the spare bedroom, preparing for her stay. 'You okay?' Kavya asked me, concerned about my sudden slump in energy. I didn't want to worry her or my mom, but I knew what was wrong. The clammy skin, the pounding head, the dry mouth. The shaking and agitation I felt. I needed a drink; no, wanted a drink. It had been days since I had last touched alcohol, and somehow, my body and mind had forgotten how to function without it.

'Do you know what I need right now?'

'What?' She eyed me suspiciously.

'Some of that junk you force-fed me to feel better about yourself,' I said and grinned. She threw a cushion at me, which I dodged, giggling like a child.

'I'll go downstairs and get us some,' she said, grabbing her purse. 'Don't be laying on the floor when I get back,' she called as she walked out the door. I picked up my phone and, choosing my favourite photo of her and me together, I posted it to my account.

'Wouldn't be alive without this woman in my life.'

For the first time in a long time, what I had posted was the truth. No filters. No PR. Just the truth.

26

ASHRAY

They told me that going through grief is a process. I always wondered who they were. Had they actually experienced grief, and the 'process'?

For two days, I was stuck in a hospital bed, unable to move without paralysing chest pains. What was the point of living anyway, I thought, if everything I had worked for since high school was now laying in a morgue in the same building I was unable to leave? Maa's doctor came in to check on me, trying to reassure me that nothing I could have done would have changed things, but I knew that my actions, me not taking her to the doctor when she'd had a cold, could have meant a different outcome. I stood up from my bed and walked to the window; I needed some sun on my skin.

'Ashray.' A man in a doctor's lab coat walked into my hospital room. 'Good to see you up.' He wrote something on his chart. 'How are you feeling today?'

'Fine,' I told him, not wanting to get into the details of the guilt building inside of me.

'We're going to discharge you today with some medication, but I suggest that you see our resident psychiatrist so that you can manage your panic attacks.'

Panic attacks; I rubbed my forehead—how weak was I? It would be so much easier if there were something physically wrong with me, but the truth was that, going home, back to the apartment where my life changed, did throw me into a panic. All her things were there, our whole lives together. The pressure began to build again and I put my hand on the wall to steady myself.

'Ashray, breathe.' I tried to listen to his instruction, knowing he was a doctor, trusting that he knew what he was talking about. 'Here.' He handed me a pill, and spoke encouragingly to me until the feeling passed.

'How long are these going to last?' I asked finally, unsure that I wanted an answer.

'Panic attacks are complicated, Ashray. For many years, we thought that they were entirely psychological, but lately, we have discovered that they may be neurological as well.'

'What does that mean?'

'It means you need to take your medication and see a psychiatrist as soon as possible.' I nodded. 'So, I'm signing you out, you can leave in an hour.'

I fixed my gaze outside, on a woman walking through the parking area; her mother, father, and what might have been her sister were leaving, supporting her as they walked towards a waiting taxi. And me? I would be leaving alone. I had no one left. Absolutely nobody on earth who loved me unconditionally anymore. The only person who would care if the ground swallowed me up would be Rishi. I would need to let him know I was leaving in an hour; he was constantly messaging, trying to find out if I was coping.

'Coping'; such an ambiguous word. Was 'coping' being alive, but no longer living? Because if that was what it was, then, yes, I was coping.

I opened the overnight bag Rishi had packed three nights ago. I didn't have a set of clothes to change into, and would need to go home in my suit trousers and shirt or in the tracksuit I had been wearing for the last two days. I slipped my trousers on, buttoning up my shirt, determined to walk out of the hospital looking decent. I picked up my bag, signed out in the register and, hoping to avoid Sakshi, made my way downstairs and out the hospital doors.

The feeling of being outside was overwhelming—I felt more confined in the open than I had in my hospital room. Remembering what the doctor had said, I concentrated on my breathing. It didn't work. My heart began to pound, and blood rushed to my head. I ran to the side of the road and stuck out my hand, hoping that a taxi would stop immediately. Luckily, one did, and I flung open the car door and dove into the safe confines of the vehicle, slamming the door behind me.

'Where to?' I pulled myself out of the attack long enough to give him the address. Laying back against the seat, I closed my eyes, willing my heart to slow down and my breathing to normalise. The cab stopped at the end of my street and I got out, dreading walking past the grocer where I normally picked up Maa's free sheet. I put my head down and walked quickly past him, avoiding a conversation. I ran up the stairs of my apartment building. Without thinking, I put the key in the door and threw the door open. I tugged on my collar, desperate to free myself from the feeling of being restricted.

'I can't breathe. Can't breathe!' I screamed.

'Ashray!' The door flew open behind me. Rishi rushed into the apartment and grabbed my arms. I stuck my hand in my trouser pocket, fishing for my pills. Rishi took them from me and opened the bottle while I held my throat, gasping for breath. He handed me one; I swallowed hard, counting the seconds until they would work.

'I don't want to be here,' I turned to him and said. 'Take me away, please Rishi.' While I was in this space, I couldn't focus, couldn't heal.

'Okay, buddy, just hold on.' He ran to my room and, grabbing as many clothes as he could, he threw them into a suitcase.

'Let's go,' he said, grabbing my keys and bag. My breathing began to calm as we walked outside, and by the time we were a block away from the apartment, I felt the pressure in my chest subside.

'I don't want to go back there,' I said to him as we walked along the crowded street.

'We'll make arrangements to get everything boxed and taken over to the new place this weekend,' he said. It was the first time I had ever seen him serious. 'Until then, you can stay at my place, and Vihaan is happy for you to take some time off if you can keep your current clients happy from home.'

'Thank you,' I said, not wanting to make eye contact with him. Afraid that he would see the weakness in my eyes. I needed to make arrangements for Maa, needed to see the psychiatrist so that these attacks could stop. The bus ride to Rishi's apartment was silent. I couldn't speak; terrified that opening my mouth would set off another panic attack. I stared out of the window, focusing on the Mumbai landscape, pushing down my tears.

27

JHANVI

A turning point; those moments in our lives where we can choose one path or another. Realising that one of those paths will lead to destruction, while the other could lead to something less than the torturous existence you have found yourself in. It is difficult; veering off the path that you have been on for so long. The familiar, even if the familiar is littered with bramble thorns that tear at your flesh with every tired step that you take, is tempting. The other path, the unfamiliar, is clear, but following it may mean being lost, and that is terrifying. It is new, and new is not always easy.

Kavya walked me to the door of the psychiatrist's office, holding my arm, knowing that I wanted to flee. As she had on so many days before this—while I battled the need to numb the irritation growing inside me, when bravery took over and I boldly threw out all of the remaining alcohol in my apartment, and then when panic overtook me, when it sank in that I could never touch alcohol again—Kavya stood firm. My rock and my support. Externally, I was brave. Internally, my demons screamed that there was nothing wrong with me. I was in control of everything that happened to me.

In the psychiatrist's office, I filled in the forms as my hands shook uncontrollably. The smell of leather filled the air as I sat on the couch in the waiting room. The room was homely, modern and littered with objects that would distract or comfort, depending on what was needed.

When Kavya eventually hugged me and promised to return in an hour, I let go of the brave face I had been clinging on to. My leg began to shake, and my hands grew clammy. Cell phones weren't allowed in here, Kavya knew this, and she made sure that I had shut mine down before we even entered the room. I picked up a magazine, flipping through it quickly, but it didn't calm my mind. I shifted in my seat, crossing my legs, willing the nervous jump in my leg to stop its torturous dance. Picking up one of the cushions on the couch next to me, I clutched it tightly to my chest. My leg calmed, but my mind didn't. I was scared that the doctor would find something wrong with me, that he would agree that I needed to be separated from society until there was a sense of normality in me. I closed my eyes and breathed deeply.

'Are you all right?' The receptionist peered over the counter, making eye contact with me. 'Do you want some water?'

'No, thank you,' I managed. 'I'm just a little bit nervous.' She smiled warmly at me, no judgement from her that I could see. She must have seen people from all walks of life, nervously waiting for their first appointment.

'This is a safe space, and if you feel like you can't be out here, there is a separate room you can wait in. If you like?' I shook my head, determined to work through my nervousness, sure that I could fight the desire to flee from the confrontation that I thought was coming. As promised, my parents were keeping in touch with me more often now, and I found myself picking up the phone to call them without the need for reminders. Kavya's help in arranging my schedule alleviated a lot of pressure. But I still couldn't shake the feeling that I needed to be perfect. My life was a performance, and my audience was behind the screen of the very device that I had been forced to switch off.

I shook my head, pulling the cushion into my chest tighter. 'You can do this, Jhanvi,' I whispered, thankful that there was no one else in the room to judge me for speaking to myself. The door to the reception opened and a tall man with a panicked look on his face, burst in. He clutched the door frame, and

I could see him counting under his breath. He reached into his pocket and nervously swallowed what I thought must be medication he needed to pull himself out of the agony he was in.

The receptionist stood up but didn't move, allowing the man to try and gain control over what was happening to his body and mind. Eventually, he looked up. Sweat glistened on his forehead, which he patted away with a white handkerchief. He locked eyes with me, and I could tell he was just as terrified as I was of the path that lay in front of us. I lowered my gaze, burying my chin into the cushion, willing time to move quickly so that I could get out of here with at least some of my sanity intact.

28

ASHRAY

Rishi couldn't get time off work to accompany me to the psychiatrist's office for my first appointment. I understood, of course; it was bad enough that I was working from home until I had whatever this was under control. The panic attacks were debilitating at first, but at least they were few and far between, usually triggered by some memory or some action that reminded me of what had happened. The only place I felt safe was in my new apartment, in the place that only had one memory of my Maa.

Rishi was good to me, moving all of our belongings over and respectfully boxing Maa's things, putting them in the spare room for me to go through in my own time. I sensed, though, that he was becoming impatient with me. He wanted his friend back, and there was no way that I could explain to him that I wanted me back too. I didn't want to live in a constant state of fear that, at any given moment, my heart would begin to race, and I would lose control of myself.

Taking a bus to the doctor's office was out of the question. Panic rose the second the elevator doors closed in my apartment building, and by the time they opened in the lobby, I was fighting for my breath. Diving into a taxi, I shoved the psychiatrist's card into the taxi driver's hands before lifting my arms over my head and counting each breath I took, trying to focus on breathing in deeply and exhaling with control. It worked temporarily, but by the time we pulled up at the office, fear exploded inside me. What if the doctor told me I couldn't recover from this? What if I was broken? Permanently scarred from watching my Maa die. What if my mother, all those years ago, instinctively knew that I was defective, abandoning me in the same way an animal does when nature tells them that their offspring is not normal?

I threw the money for the journey onto the front seat of the taxi before running the short distance to the psychiatrist's office. This was nerve-wracking, going to see someone who would delve into my mind and ready me to go to war with myself. And that was the thing, Maa wasn't there anymore, she wasn't standing behind me, encouraging me, guiding me through the battle of my life. She was gone, and I felt like I would have to fight this fight alone. I must have looked a sight, bursting into the silent room, hands fumbling for the pills that kept me sane. I counted my breaths, willing the rushing blood to calm and for my hands to be steady so I could find my mouth and administer the antidote for the war raging inside me. As I felt the panic dissipate, I looked up. A woman, familiar and scared-looking, sat on a large leather couch, a cushion clutched so tightly to her chest that her knuckles were white. She looked at me wide-eyed, not judging, but sympathetic. Understanding.

'Has it passed?' the woman at the reception desk asked me. I nodded, realising that the woman sitting on the couch meant that I was not completely alone in this world. I handed the receptionist my hospital referral, and she smiled warmly as she passed me some forms. 'If you need to be alone, there is a separate room for you to wait in,' she said as I dabbed away the sweat that was pooling on my forehead.

'No, thank you.' I wanted to be close to the woman on the couch, not to speak to her, but for the comfort she didn't know she was giving me. For the knowledge that I was not alone, and that if she could be here, bravely fighting what was happening inside her, then so could I. I sat on the couch opposite her and began to fill in the forms methodically, making sure that nothing was missed.

'Jhanvi,' the receptionist said, 'the doctor will see you now. Do you want to take that with you?' She pointed at the cushion the woman was clinging to. She nodded as she stood up, and was led through to another room. For a moment, I thought she would leave the clinic, her comforter clutched to her chest, but, one foot in front of the other, she made her way out of the reception area and into the rooms behind me.

The receptionist looked at me. 'Don't leave, okay? You're a little early, but you are safe here.'

I shook my head. I couldn't leave if I tried, I thought. My body wouldn't allow it. The panic was already fast taking hold again, and once it did, there would be nothing I could do until it subsided.

I nodded my head, managing a weak smile.

I don't know what I expected walking into the doctor's office for the first time. For days, I had allowed my imagination to run away with me, expecting him to be a stern man in a clinical room. Instead, the room was warmly decorated, and waiting for me at the door was what could only be described as a fatherly looking man. I looked around, taking in my surroundings. This would be a good place for a photo, I thought. I couldn't help it; I was constantly looking for a new place to create material.

'Jhanvi.' He put out his hand, a warm smile on his face. I clutched the cushion to my chest but managed to extend one hand to greet him. 'Please have a seat wherever you are comfortable.' Was this a test? Was he going to monitor and take note of where I felt most comfortable? 'You can relax, Jhanvi, this isn't a test,' he said, as if reading my mind. Maybe all his patients thought it was a test. I nodded and sat on a two-seater couch opposite two single seats.

'How are you?' he asked.

'Fine,' I replied automatically, not sure what he wanted to hear.

'Tell me, why are you here?' he said. I appreciated that he wasn't wasting time or treating me with kid gloves.

I didn't know where to begin really. 'I collapsed at home,' I said finally.

'And what caused the collapse?'

'I ... um ...' I didn't want to sound like an addict, it wasn't like I was still dependent on the alcohol and diet pills now, '... I worked too much, drank and took pills to cope. It just got out of control.'

'I see,' he said, making a note.

'Sorry,' I interrupted him, 'why are you taking notes?'

'Does it worry you?' he asked, putting his pen down. How could I respond to that without looking like I was paranoid? 'Everything that we discuss here is completely confidential, no one else will ever know about it.' I looked away from him, avoiding eye contact, avoiding conflict.

'It's fine,' I said. It didn't feel fine, but did I really have a choice?

'In the same way you are fine?' He was good.

'What?' I feigned confusion to his response.

'When you walked in here, I asked you how you were, you replied fine. But you aren't here because you're fine, Jhanvi. The only way this is going to work is if you're honest with me, okay?'

'I don't want to seem crazy,' I said, clutching the cushion to my chest. 'I'm not crazy.'

'Nobody is saying you're crazy, Jhanvi. Every person out there who is living in today's times is filled with some form of pain, is damaged in some way. Some people are just far better at concealing it or dealing with it. That doesn't make you a better or a worse person than they are, it just means that something has happened that has caused you to take a step backwards. Together, we are going to make sure you can move forward again without relapsing.' I couldn't hold back my tears any longer, couldn't stop the flood gates from opening.

'I need to be perfect. Need to be in control,' I sobbed. 'Without control, my life … this life I have created … will fall apart, and I can't let that happen because if I do, then what am I? What is my purpose outside of what I have created?' He handed me a box of tissues, allowing me to compose myself. For the remainder of the session, we spoke about why I felt the need to control every aspect of my life. By the end of the session, I felt that my parents insisting on me coming here was probably the best thing they could have done. Walking out of the room, I felt lighter, a little clearer about the direction I should take. I placed the cushion back on the couch and smiled at the man still fidgeting with his collar.

As I left the psychiatrist's office, I switched on my phone and posted a photo from one of my afternoon walks before all of this happened. Hearts filled my screen once again, but this time, it didn't feel like I needed them.

By our seventh session together, I began to understand why Dr Shyam asked the questions he did. Addictive personality disorder, that was my label, and we were working on becoming healthy, finding ways for me to not fixate and rely on external stimuli to feel content. Dr Shyam insisted I stop calling it a label. I was not an object. Regardless, I couldn't see it as anything other than that I was broken. Defective.

'And how many times a day are you checking your social media statistics?' he asked, making sure to make eye contact with me.

'Less than before,' I answered, knowing that breaking eye contact with him would be a tell that I was lying.

'Don't avoid answering the question, Jhanvi. Remember that direct answers are the only answers that are allowed here.' I rolled my eyes at him, far more comfortable with showing him my true feelings now. He had broken through, past my tough exterior. He could see me for all of me. I could be here, just be. Exploring who I am and who I wanted to become.

I relented. 'Four or five times a day,' I said.

'Or?'

I flopped back into the two-seater couch, folding my arms and pouting. He always asked more questions to get the full truth.

'Or whenever I'm bored.' I looked out of the window, knowing that this was against the rules.

'And how often are you getting bored?'

'Look, Kavya is helping me a lot with my schedule. She practically controls every aspect of my life, so I'm not exactly busy all the time anymore, and I get bored. A lot.'

'So, you're relinquishing control more often then?' I shrugged, knowing this was what he was aiming for. Our last few sessions had been all about my need to control almost every aspect of my life. 'Jhanvi, I don't think you're allowing Kavya to control your schedule or your life. I think you feed her the information you want her to hear so that she can fit you into a schedule you already have in mind. And if something goes wrong? Well, then you don't have to take responsibility for it because you have Kavya to fall back on.' I sat open-mouthed, unable to talk. 'Think about it,' he said and looked at his watch. 'We'll discuss it at our next session.' I walked out of his office, confused, perhaps angry. In the waiting room, the man who couldn't breathe sat reading some papers. I smiled at him; he had become a regular feature in my life, and it was good to see that he seemed to be improving. This was the third session he had been able to walk into the office without having to take his pills.

'Would you like to meet me after your session for coffee?' I asked, inwardly shocked at myself for doing something so rash. He stared at me, unsure of how to respond. 'I mean, no strings attached, I just thought it might be nice to have a friend who understands all of this.' I turned around to leave.

'No, sorry,' he said as he stood up from the couch. 'It's just, this kind of thing doesn't happen all that often. I'm Ashray.' He extended his hand. I shook it, expecting his palms to be damp, but they weren't, and he didn't break eye contact with me.

'Jhanvi. I'll see you outside in forty-five minutes,' I said and waved bye, still shocked at my actions but not regretting that I may have made a new friend.

30

ASHRAY

The woman with the mesmerising eyes walked out of the doctor's office. Her face seemed familiar, and I wondered briefly if maybe we had crossed paths somewhere before, but my mind was too tired to remember anything. I noticed that she was looking less anxious, and that gave me hope that the psychiatrist could help me gain control of what was happening to me. I saw that she had even let go of the cushion she had been holding so tightly to her chest when I first walked in. I didn't have a cushion; perhaps I should have tried her soothing technique, because I felt the familiar pain in my chest driving me into another attack at the thought of going through to see the doctor. The woman stood at the receptionist's desk, confirming her next appointment before leaving the room. Before the door closed behind her, her face was buried in her phone. Why couldn't I distract myself in the same way others did? And why hadn't she done it before, when she quite clearly needed to be distracted? I looked around and noticed the sign that cell phones weren't allowed in the reception area. Quickly, I reached for mine and switched it off. My hands shook uncontrollably.

'Stop it,' I whispered, close to tears.

'Ashray, the doctor will see you now.' The receptionist walked out from behind her desk with a file that held the forms I had filled in earlier. I tugged on my collar, sure that I was going to be told there was something drastically wrong with me. A pine door opened. Inside, the room was decorated in a way I am sure my Maa would have loved. Burgundy and blues added touches of colour to a room filled with wood and leather. Dr Shyam stood at the door, hand outstretched. I wiped my hand on my trouser leg, wanting to spare a stranger from the clamminess of my palms. I shook his hand.

'Take a seat anywhere you're comfortable,' he said, indicating the couches in the room. I tugged on my collar.

'Ashray, are you okay?'

I pulled the pills out of my pocket before realising that I had taken one less than an hour ago. I put them back and lifted my hands above my head, trying to breathe deeply.

'Ashray,' he said as he put his hand on my shoulder, 'you don't need the pill, not now.' I counted as I breathed in, but I felt like I didn't have the strength to let it out again. 'Ashray look at me.' I willed my eyes to meet his. 'Tell me five things you can see right now.' I looked at him, shocked. Was this man serious? I was in the middle of a panic attack! I couldn't breathe, and he wanted me to tell him what I could see. 'Ashray. Tell me five things you can see,' he tried again calmly.

'A rug, a—.'

'No,' he interrupted me, 'with details, please.' More pain pressed on my chest. I tried to focus, tried to work through what was happening to me.

'A burgundy rug,' I managed finally.

'Good, continue please.'

'A wooden desk, a black office chair, a leather couch and a large bookshelf,' I rushed through the list of things I could see, wondering what the point of this was.

'Good. Now four things you can hear.'

'A clock, the wind, traffic, um,' I stopped for a second, trying to focus, 'a phone. I hear a phone.'

'Great, Ashray. Now, three things you can smell right now.' My confusion grew, but I felt like I should comply.

'My cologne, the leather from the couches, and coffee.'

'How are you feeling, Ashray?' I was bewildered, unable to understand what was happening. 'Ashray, are you still having a panic attack?' I shook my head, shocked that something so simple had worked that quickly.

'No … no, I'm not.'

'Good,' he said. 'Should we try this again? Please have a seat anywhere you're comfortable.' I sat on the two-seater couch, where I was sure the woman who was in here before had sat. It seemed comfortable. Safe.

'What brings you here today?' he asked. I leaned back and moaned. What hadn't brought me here today?

'Would you like to meet me for coffee after your session?' the woman who had become the reason for me to come to therapy asked. I didn't know how to respond initially. Dr Shyam and I were working on me being less dependent, less attached to the people who came into my life. I was worried that I wasn't quite at the stage where I would be able to accept an invite from her without becoming dependent on her. She was incredibly beautiful and, over the course of her sessions, I could see that she was beginning to find her way again. Long gone was the woman who had clutched a cushion to her chest. And me? I still had panic attacks, but through the doctor's grounding techniques, I was able to manage them a lot better. Although not all the techniques worked, and sometimes those that did usually work failed to pull me out of a full-blown attack, I had reached a point where I was able to return to work, return to some semblance of normality.

I followed the receptionist through to the doctor's room, in the same way that I had for the last few weeks. Dr Shyam was waiting for me at the door, hand outstretched. He was constant, the same way my Maa had been, and I often thought that perhaps I had found another crutch. Another person to latch onto.

Towards the end of the session, he said, 'So, I wanted to talk about your relationship with Sakshi.' I wasn't ready for this, wasn't ready to open up about why her betrayal cut so deep.

'There's nothing to talk about,' I said, hoping to cut the conversation short before it could begin.

'But I think there is. Why did her leaving make you feel the way you did?'

'Isn't it normal to feel heartbroken when someone you love rejects you?'

'Rejection is a strong word, Ashray. Why do you feel that she rejected you specifically?'

'Well, she isn't here, is she?' I shot back, irritated with his line of questioning.

'But did she reject you or did she choose to avoid conflict with her parents? How do you know that her pain wasn't just as real as yours?' I stared at him, unwilling to answer his question. 'Ashray, do you understand that choosing to obey her parents' wishes does not mean she rejected you. It just means that she made a choice for her life. A choice that possibly meant an incredible amount of sacrifice for her.'

'She didn't even contact me after the night she broke up with me. Not once!' I shouted.

'Anger is good, Ashray but don't you think it is misplaced?' I didn't think it was. I thought I was completely justified in being angry with her. 'There are no right or wrong answers, Ashray.'

'No. No, I don't think that my anger is misplaced! She left me. Used me while she tried to decide whether she would obey her parents, and when she decided it was too difficult to love me without their approval, she threw me away. Like a piece of rubbish. A broken toy. She threw me away, just like—' I cut off, not wanting to speak about it anymore.

'Just like who?' I shook my head. Not prepared to go any further. 'Just like who, Ashray?' He leaned forward in his chair. He did that when he knew we were getting somewhere.

'Just like my mother, okay?'

'Good, Ashray. That is progress, and I think it is enough for today.' I nodded, irritated that our session had ended with me having to rehash my feelings of rejection once again. Especially since I was meeting Jhanvi after my session.

'Thanks,' I said, walking towards the door. 'I'll see you next week.' I walked out of the office and into the reception area to make my next appointment. On the couch, a young woman sat, crouched over, rocking. I smiled. So much could change in a short amount of time, and not all of it was bad.

31

JHANVI

'Hi,' I called out, waving to Ashray as he walked out of the clinic. I'd spent the forty-five minutes he was in his session sitting on a bench in the shade, updating my feed and sending messages back and forth to Kavya to try and arrange shoots for the week. My numbers were slowly starting to recover, which was good, but I would admit that I found myself a little distracted again. The fact that Kavya and I wanted to move into a new apartment seemed to drive me further into my need to control every aspect of my life. She was so strong in supporting me, I simply couldn't let her down, and my apartment really was too small for both of us.

Ashray walked towards me, irritation on his face. It took me a moment to understand that his expression wasn't one of fighting another panic attack. He truly was annoyed. Perhaps Dr Shyam had pushed his buttons today as well. 'Tough session?' I asked, genuinely concerned, but unable to pull my face from my screen until I had a screenshot of my statistics.

'You could say that.' He hovered over me, his brown briefcase in hand. I put my phone away.

'Me too,' I said.

'There are just some things I'm not ready to talk about,' he said, clearly still annoyed with the doctor's line of questioning.

'I know, right?' I said, relieved that someone finally understood that as much as these sessions were working, helping me come back from the brink of self-destruction, they were also tough and often took me to a place I wasn't comfortable with. 'So, what button did he push?' I asked, and then immediately wondered whether I was overstepping the line. I shrugged, trying to dismiss my last sentence, but instead of being offended, he laughed at my awkwardness.

'He wants me to deal with my abandonment issues,' he said and rolled his eyes.

'Fantastic. I'm a control freak who is manipulating my best friend.' He stared at me wide-eyed. I burst out laughing, knowing how ridiculously juvenile I sounded.

'So, my Maa died, and I ended up in the same hospital on the same day as she died because of a panic attack,' he continued, 'but I blame my ex.'

'What did she do?'

'Strung me along. Waited for me to fall in love with her and then told me that our relationship was over because she had to marry someone chosen for her.'

'What?' I was genuinely surprised.

'Yup. So, now, I am alone with abandonment issues and a tendency to fixate on anyone that pays me any attention.'

'And your dad?'

'I don't have one. I'm an orphan. My Maa adopted me, so there is no one else.'

I put my hand on his shoulder to comfort him. I had all of these people in my life, real and virtual, but I felt alone for the most part, and here was Ashray. Someone who really was alone, still somehow coping. Keeping his head above water.

He continued. 'And with these panic attacks, I think it's safe to say that I will be alone forever. Collapsing in a sweaty, messy ball isn't exactly marriage material.'

Looking at this man, hearing his story, encouraged me. My problems seemed so small compared to his. He was inspirational, and I was grateful that I had dared to introduce myself to him. 'What about you?' he asked.

'Not nearly as dramatic as you. I'm moderately famous—'

'Famous?' he interrupted me.

'Moderately,' I said. 'Anyway, I found out that my second boyfriend in a row was cheating on me, I overworked, started drinking to overcome the exhaustion and eventually isolated everyone in my life until I collapsed in my living room and almost died.'

'Almost dying is pretty dramatic,' he said and smiled at me.

'I guess, but I mean, I still have people in my life. It's just that sometimes I wish they would just let me prove that I can do this by myself.'

'Why would you want to be alone?' he asked, genuinely curious. Feelings of guilt welled inside me when I remembered that he didn't have anyone to lean on.

'I don't know,' I said, not really understanding why I felt the way I did. 'I guess I feel this need to be perfect.'

'Nothing is perfect, Jhanvi.'

'What do you mean?'

He held up his briefcase, the one I had been eyeing for a few sessions now, imagining all the photos I could take with it. 'What do you think of this?'

'It's beautiful! So retro and worn, I love it! I would totally use it in one of my shoots.' He nodded his head, seeming to agree with me.

'So, you would say it is perfect then?'

'Yes,' I agreed, not understanding where he was going with this.

'This briefcase is older than me. I detest it because it is old, it's a sign that I haven't quite made it in life yet; but to you, it is perfect.'

'So why do you keep it?' I asked, trying to understand what he was getting at.

'Because it reminds me of where I have come from. The point is, I won't get rid of it because I am attached and sentimental, but I do not see it in the same way that you do.'

'You're quite profound,' I said, staring at my feet. 'And you are not alone. ' I looked up at him, making sure that he understood. 'You have me now.'

'Be careful, Jhanvi, I might get too attached,' he said, smiling at me.

'I wouldn't mind,' I replied.

And I didn't mind. At least he understood me.

32

ASHRAY

Jhanvi was waiting for me outside, in the same way she had been for the last four sessions.

Soon after my first session at the clinic, I remembered where I had first met Jhanvi. At first I thought I would tell her that we had met before, but I changed my mind—I didn't think she would remember anything about that eventful night at the Goa Music Festival, where she got wasted. In any case, it didn't make any sense to bring that memory back to her when she was trying to recover. So I decided never to talk about it.

I liked Jhanvi; liked that she seemed to understand what was going through my mind and that she listened to me without judgement. Slowly, I was able to reintroduce myself back at the office. Vihaan was wonderful, supporting me however he could, and Rishi did his part, but neither of them truly understood what was going on inside me. The terrifying feelings that overtook me when I was alone. Jhanvi got that. She understood that, no matter how many people surrounded you, you could still feel utterly alone in the world.

'You ready for our stroll?' I asked Jhanvi. She had her eyes glued to her screen, worrying about something yet again. I saw the internal struggle she had just trying to pull her eyes away from her phone.

'Yeah,' she responded, putting her phone in her bag and zipping it shut.

'How has the week been?' she asked, standing up from the bench.

'Okay. Work is going great.'

'I don't mean work, Ashray, you know that.'

'I've been good,' I said, 'really. No panic attacks and the loneliness at night has been manageable.'

'Then, what is preoccupying your mind?' She knew me so well already.

'Just before Maa …' I couldn't say the words yet, '… well, before she left, I signed a lease on my dream apartment. It was meant to be a place that she could grow old in, but now, it just seems too big. Too empty for just me.' She nodded, listening intently to what I was saying.

'So, what are you going to do?'

'I don't know.' I really didn't know yet. 'Just the thought of moving again, having to take her stuff somewhere else, makes me feel anxious.'

'Then stay a little longer, until you feel like you can,' she said, patting my arm.

'It's her birthday next week. My Maa's.'

'Ashray, I'm sorry, do you have anyone to be with you?' I shook my head, knowing that Rishi and Latika would be there if I asked them, but I didn't know if I wanted to share my grief. Didn't know if I would even grieve.

'I don't want anyone around. I feel like it might be a good exercise in learning how to be alone.'

'What does Dr Shyam say?' she asked, like she instinctively knew there was a gap in my story.

'He doesn't know Jhanvi, and I don't want him to. Nobody knows except you and me, okay?'

'Okay,' she replied, her dark brown eyes burning into me, searching for a sign that I was going to be all right. 'But if you feel like you can't handle it, even for a second, you call me, okay?' I agreed, feeling better about the upcoming birthday and my newfound strength to tackle it alone.

'What about you?'

'What about me?' she mocked me, locking her arm into mine. I rolled my eyes at her, pretending to be annoyed.

'Kavya is irritating me,' she admitted. 'Not on purpose, mind you. She is just doing what I asked her to do, but sometimes I want to do things for myself. I find myself wanting to drink again. To do something to take my mind off everything that is stressing me out right now ...' she trailed off.

'But she is still acting on your instructions?' She nodded at my question. 'Well, then, aren't you indirectly doing it yourself then?'

'You're infuriating,' she said, frowning at me.

'I know.' I puffed out my chest, exaggerating a sense of pride. She reached into her bag, pulling out her phone.

'Selfie?' I laughed, but agreed to share the moment with her. She angled her face, posing with perfection. For a brief moment, it felt like I was standing with someone I barely knew. She opened her gallery to review the pictures. Staring back at me was the two of us, her looking absolutely magnificent as always, and me, somehow with the most ridiculous half-smile imaginable.

'Sorry,' I said, truly apologetic. She wrinkled her nose, a smile that reached all the way to her eyes.

'I like it,' she answered. 'I think it is the perfect picture.' We walked together, arm in arm, a little while longer.

'How does this whole "moderately famous" thing work?' I asked her. No response as she flicked between screens with graphs and words I didn't understand. 'Jhanvi?'

'Something is wrong, my stats have never been this slow. I think they've changed the algorithm again.' I looked at her, struggling to separate her self-worth from what was happening behind her screen, sure that this would mean a setback for her. Reaching over, I gently took the phone from her hand before locking it and putting it in my pocket.

'That's enough of that for now, hey?' Her initial reaction of shock made me think that I had overstepped the boundary, but eventually, her expression softened.

'All right,' she said, 'you can give it back when Kavya comes to fetch me.' I listened to her try and explain how her world worked, but all I heard was the enormous pressure to perform, the inability to have a bad day. I felt for her, understood why she would feel the need to be perfect, but I also wanted her to understand that perfection would never be attainable. Not in today's disposable world. She was passionate about her life, but somewhere, her ideals had become skewed. If only she could understand that the real Jhanvi, the woman walking arm in arm with me right now, was what the world needed to see. She could be selective and still make an impact. Looking up at me, I could sense her longing, a longing I knew too well. To be accepted and loved with the knowledge that, that love wouldn't be thrown away or betrayed by those who claimed to love us back.

'So your friend, Rishi, he's dating someone?' she asked suddenly.

I eyed her suspiciously.

'You looking for a boyfriend?' I asked, half joking.

'Oh no! Dr Shyam doesn't think that is the greatest idea right now. I was actually thinking about Kavya. Perhaps if she had a man in her life, she would give me more freedom.'

'You're impossible.' I laughed, pulling her into my side.

'I know,' she replied, 'but really. Is he seeing someone?' I gathered that she was trying to find out if there was a reason for me not wanting to burden Rishi with the fact that it was my Maa's birthday. Honestly, I didn't want to have the conversation, but there was something about her. Perhaps it was the fact that we were both wounded, trying to heal an invisible pain that we felt others could not possibly understand. Or maybe it was her vulnerability and the fact that I felt safe being vulnerable with her.

'He has a girlfriend, they have been together a while now.' I pulled out my phone to show her a picture of Rishi. Her mouth fell open.

'I know this woman!'

'What?' I couldn't believe we had someone in common in our lives.

'She's my cheating ex-boyfriend's ex-girlfriend. Complicated, I know.' She grinned at me. I shook my head in disbelief.

'Are you sure?'

She laughed at me and I understood why. There was no way that anyone could mistake Latika.

'She is actually a friend of mine. I … um …' She stopped, recalling something that was difficult for her to express. 'She was with me the night of the club opening, the night I got sick.' I looked at her, understanding what it meant to avoid using the words that admitted there was something more than physical illness happening with us.

'I'm glad she was with you,' I replied, not wanting to push for more details. Latika was a lot to handle, but she was a good person, a reliable friend, and I was glad that Jhanvi had someone like her in her life.

Just then, her friend Kavya pulled up in a taxi. I leaned over and kissed Jhanvi on the cheek, promising to call her if I felt there was anything I couldn't handle and making her promise the same. Although I knew that her need to control her life, her fear of failure, would mean that she wouldn't. I cared for her in a way that was different to how I had felt about Sakshi. I had no expectations of her, but I did hope. Hope that, with time and with healing, we could find a middle ground. Somewhere between the comfort we felt together and a deep love that would never fade. She took her phone from me, greeting her friend warmly, but I could see it, the monster rising inside of her.

'The only thing you can do is be there for her, Ashray,' I told myself as I jumped into a taxi that would take me to the emptiness of my home.

33

JHANVI

No one ever fully recovers. Recovery is a process, ongoing and always changing. The things that set you off before become irrelevant and other things become important; life will always have something else that it throws at you. Challenging you to rise or daring you to crumble. Resting is not a sin, hiding for a little while to recover, regroup and find the strength to move forward again is fine, but hiding forever? That isn't an option. That isn't a recovery, it is defeat, and defeat isn't an option when you love yourself.

'You cannot fit anything else into your schedule, Jhanvi.' Kavya was pushing back at my insistence that I needed to get more done to bring my figures back up to where they had been. I was irritated, battling more than one addiction, and my body continued to try and force me to relapse. I used positive reinforcement every day, but some days I needed to repeatedly tell myself that I was beautiful and loved. Today was one of those days that I felt I needed a mirror attached to my hand, to remind myself that I was capable of overcoming everything right now.

'I only need to see Dr Shyam once a week from here on, so that is forty-five minutes freed up.' She looked at me suspiciously, not prepared to budge. She had become an immovable hindrance in my pursuit of perfection, and I didn't know whether I loved her or hated her for it. I didn't share my withdrawal pains with Kavya, nor did I let her know that there were moments where I felt that my skin was on fire and the only thing that could, or would, put it out was one of the objects I used for my own personal high. Distraction wasn't working, affirmations seemed to occasionally. But the burn was intense, and it did not seem like the fire would be suffocated any other way.

'Your mom called again as well,' she said, holding my phone up for me to see the three missed calls. I rolled my eyes. 'Jhanvi, phone them please, and have a real conversation with them. They are worried about you.' I took my phone, promising to call them in the morning after some rest.

How was I supposed to rest, heal, if everyone wanted a piece of me? I felt like I was being pulled in too many directions again and I didn't like it. Didn't like the feeling of what little control I had left in my life being stripped away from me. I closed my bedroom door behind me, telling Kavya I was tired. I wasn't lying, I felt exhausted, and I didn't know why. Perhaps it was the constant fight against my own body; it felt as if my soul was tired. Lying down on the bed, I fell asleep quickly. Avoiding my emotions right now just seemed easier than tackling them head-on. A little sleep never hurt anyone. Besides, not enough sleep was what had caused all of my issues before.

'Jhanvi?' Kavya knocked on my door, waking me from my sleep. 'Your appointment with Dr Shyam is in two hours,' she said tentatively.

'I'll reschedule,' I said, rolling over so that I didn't have to look at her.

'Are you okay?'

'I don't feel well,' I said, trying to sound convincing. The truth was I felt fine, physically at least. Mentally, I was exhausted from trying to find out what was happening with my social media account, from having to plaster a smile on my face all the time, pretending that everything was fine. Her hand brushed my hair from my face. 'Kavya, please, just let me be for a bit, okay? Everyone complains I work too much, and now that I am taking a break, everyone expects me to get up and be busy.'

'I don't expect that of you, Jhanvi, I'm just concerned.'

'I know, just let me rest, please.' She left the room, closing the door behind her. I rolled my eyes, annoyed with myself for snapping at her. I closed my eyes again, allowing sleep to pull me into avoidance. Avoidance of my life, avoidance of my family, avoidance of getting better. Sleep was safe, everything else required me to use energy I didn't have. The truth was that I preferred to stay in my sleep; here, I didn't need to wake up to the nightmare my life had become. I didn't need to battle my addiction. My life was a nightmare, one that I will admit that I had created. And sleep? Sleep was my safe place, away from the demons that chased me in my waking hours.

Voices in my house. A man's voice. Was my father here? My bedside clock told me it was a quarter to five in the evening. I would normally be finishing my walk with Ashray now. Ashray. I oriented myself, recognising the voice as his. I must be dreaming, had to be imagining him in my home. He didn't know where I lived. I rolled over, looking for my phone so that I could type him a message. He worried about so much, I didn't want him worrying about me too. My phone wasn't in its usual spot; Kavya must have taken it to schedule appointments. I groaned—as if more appointments were what I needed right now. A tentative knock on my door. I ignored it before realising that, to get my phone back, I would need to speak to Kavya.

'Yes,' I managed, my back still turned to the door.

I heard the door open slowly, and Ashray's voice broke the silence.

'Are you decent?' I sighed, not wanting to deal with anyone right now.

'Yes.' He walked into my bedroom, looking around at the room decorated in white and gold.

'Nice place you have here,' he said, trying to remain casual. 'You weren't at Dr Shyam's today?'

'I don't feel well,' I told him.

'Yeah, I don't feel well either, a lot of the time.'

I was sure he would be smiling softly. I sat up in bed, knowing there was no way I could avoid this conversation with him.

'I don't know what's wrong with me, Ashray. I am just so tired all the time.'

'I think it's called being human,' he replied, trying to lighten the mood.

'Something is wrong with my account, I don't know what it is, and everyone wants a piece of me. It's exhausting.'

'Everyone wants a piece of you, or are you giving everyone a piece of you? It's okay to say no sometimes, Jhanvi.' His eyes searched mine for some sign that I understood what he was saying.

'How am I supposed to say no, Ashray? Look at this schedule, all these people who want to work with me.'

'It's quite simple: en-oh. No.' It wasn't that simple, it never was. Saying no meant rejecting people, pushing them out of my life, and that was part of the problem, wasn't it? Part of me being detached. 'Jhanvi, look at me,' he said, as he squeezed my hand. 'When are you happiest? When you are taking photos? When you are posting them? When you are with Kavya, me, your family?' I thought about it for a moment, but I knew the answer.

'When I am with my friends and family,' I answered.

'Do you know why?' I shook my head. 'Because you are present. You are here with us. With people who care about you. All of this,' he waved the phone in my face, 'it's just noise. Smoke and mirrors that give you the illusion of happiness. A temporary high that just so happens to put food on your table.

You have to learn to detach from it. You have to understand that it is no different from my nine to six job. Do you understand?' I lowered my gaze, knowing that what he was saying was true. 'Come on, get up. Kavya has made us something to eat. I told her I was starving when we spoke earlier,' he said.

'Could we lay here just a little longer,' I said, not wanting this moment with him to end.

He swung his legs onto my bed and put his arm around me, kissing the top of my head. I put my head on his chest; I felt safe. We lay together like that for a while, not saying anything, his words playing over in my head and his heartbeat soothing my pain. It felt like an eternity, those few minutes that we lay in my bed, but the moment he made a move to stand up, it also felt like a fleeting second in time. He patted his legs, and I laughed at him. Swinging my legs out of bed, I stretched, and then we walked down the passage where Kavya waited for us.

'Hi,' she said gently.

'Hi,' I replied, smiling at her, appreciating her for being in my life.

34

KAVYA

When someone you love is in pain, it transfers over to you. An intangible thread of hurt that binds the two of you in an unspoken truth. That truth is that no one can ever fully heal without accepting help from others, and accepting the need to be whole once more.

For me, with Jhanvi, the journey has been a long one. If I am to be honest, her need for control, her pursuit of perfection began young and probably through no fault of her own. She was always fiercely competitive, her brain matching her beauty, and her drive to succeed only hindered by how many hours she had in her day. I loved her, not for who she had become, but for the little girl who became my sister. It wasn't unusual for us to fight as sisters do, but our last fight was different. Instinctively I knew that something was wrong, something deep and dark was clawing at her spirit, but I couldn't force her to speak to me. Couldn't will her to be honest with me about her addiction. She needed to do that on her own, and it tore me apart, knowing that she was at home, probably lost in a sea of imagined commitments that she couldn't say no to.

When I saw her posts, saw what those women had to say about her, my sister, saw the pain in her bloodshot eyes, my gut stirred. It told me she needed me, told me that the thread that bound us would be broken, perhaps forever, if I didn't reach out.

She was stubborn, too stubborn to admit that she was out of her depth. The Jhanvi I knew, that competitive, driven little girl, would rather drown than reach out her hand. And then it happened; I found her clinging to life, her heart frantically trying to keep up with the pace she had set for herself. Fear ripped through me when I found her on the floor. Her apartment echoed the chaos that was inside her, bottles and promotional items were scattered everywhere, and the smell of unwashed dishes and rotting food assaulted my senses. When she awoke in hospital, seemingly no worse-off for what had happened to her, I knew better. Knew that her recovery would be a long, hard process; but if her determination was redirected, it could be done. I saw the pain in her parents' eyes, but more importantly, I saw something in her. Something that I had never seen before: an urgent need that said she needed help. That she needed to know that she was loved unconditionally.

She and I had good days and bad days after that. I pushed back relentlessly against her resistance, but when she went to bed and didn't want to come out, when the lights went out and the drive seemed to leave her, I realised something. I couldn't do this alone. Couldn't help keep her afloat while she fought to go under. I liked Ashray; he was good for her, even if I was sceptical to begin with. He offered her a gentleness when I had to be firm, and he didn't know her history beyond what she told him. I knew he was in pain himself, but somehow the two of them seemed to heal each other, and he brought a spark to her eyes that I had never seen before.

I was hesitant to call him, worried that he may be fighting his own demons that evening, but he didn't hesitate to come to her, to hold her and pull her out of whatever it was that had taken hold of her this time. The best I could do was watch and wait for her to emerge from the darkness. To have faith in a man that I barely knew, to be the lifeboat for both of us. There was something human about him, a proof that being a person meant that, in some way or another, we were all dealing with something that threatened to separate our sanity from our minds. And so he came to our rescue and she came out of her darkness, slightly stronger, a little more willing to continue her fight.

While we ate the meal that I had promised Ashray, Jhanvi smiled. A genuine smile. One I hadn't seen in far too many years. One that reached her eyes and brightened her face and gave me hope that the little girl inside her, my sister who I loved, was still in there and on the path back out into the world.

35

ASHRAY

Getting through the day was challenging—knowing that today was Maa's birthday, knowing that no one other than Jhanvi and I knew about it. I did my best to make small talk with Rishi. But my mind was on what I was going to do when I got home. Nothing that I could do would honour her life in a way that mattered enough to show the impact she had on me. I convinced myself that it would have been easier if she had left after her birthday. At least I would have had the chance to recover then, a few months, maybe more, to adjust to not having her in my life anymore.

To the rest of the world my grieving was over; there were no tears left to shed, not for those who spent their time around me. But the worst kind of pain doesn't manifest itself in external tears, but in the tears that come from your soul. The type that shatter your heart, fragmenting the person you once were.

Taking the bus home was a mistake; the feeling of panic all too familiar and uncomfortable. The pressure on my chest began almost the second the bus started to move. I ran my hands over my briefcase, taking in the texture, trying to remain conscious and aware of my surroundings. It didn't seem to work. Five senses, I told myself. Recounting what I saw, heard, smelled, felt and touched, over and over again, stopped the attack, but I could still feel it inside me, pounding its fists on my soul, demanding to be let out. Going home was a mistake, I knew this. Knew that I should have scheduled an appointment with Dr Shyam, but we were working on being more independent, on taking control and making my own decisions. Learning how to be comfortable in my own company. How weak would I look if I booked a third appointment for the week, just because it was Maa's birthday?

I opened my door, set my keys on the side table the way I used to when we were in the old apartment, and removed my jacket, tie and shoes at the door. I felt the cold tiles through my socks and breathed in, willing myself to be present. Putting my briefcase on the kitchen counter, I walked through to the balcony doors, opening them wide. A cool breeze filtered into the apartment and the Mumbai skyline glittered in hues of orange and gold against the black night sky. Perhaps I should have bought a table for the outside? The one she wanted. Invited Rishi over for dinner, similar to the one we had the night everything fell apart. My grief still felt too personal, too raw to share though. What if I fell apart? Would Rishi still want to be in my life if he saw that I was still broken?

The house was quiet, too quiet, but I didn't want to switch on the television; it reminded me of Maa. Didn't want to eat anything that she used to prepare for us. Right now, I didn't want to exist in a world that didn't have her in it. The pressure on my chest began to weigh me down, reminding me that no amount of avoidance could distract me from the fact that she was gone. Forever. I needed something, anything that would remind me that she had existed. That her presence on earth was meaningful and lasting. That there wasn't just this empty void where she used to be. I walked down the passage and opened the door to the spare bedroom. Three boxes in the corner of the room were filled with her things. Three boxes? Was that the sum total of what my Maa's life was? An empty room and three cardboard boxes? The blood started rushing in. I opened one box and the sweet smell of incense filled the room. My Maa had preferred jasmine incense over sandalwood. The familiar smell made me smile, but my heart felt that it would crack. A small wooden box with lotus flowers engraved on them beckoned me. Inside it was an envelope and in her handwriting, a note:

'*Ashray's birthday present.*'

My breathing quickened. This was a bad idea, I told myself; I shouldn't be doing this, I wasn't ready. But my fingers were already tearing the envelope open. Inside, the roll of money I had handed back to her after my weekend at the Goa Music Festival was neatly flattened; a paperclip held it together, along with a note of how much was there.

The attack didn't grow slowly this time. There was no way I could have used any of the techniques that the doctor had taught me. Like a flash flood, it swelled and consumed everything in its path almost instantaneously. I couldn't breathe, couldn't focus, had no idea where my pills were. My hands shook violently as I searched my pockets, but the only thing I could find was my phone. Not much good that was. I was alone. Completely alone! In this house. In my life. I was alone. I pulled my phone out, preparing to throw it, not sure if I was even coordinated enough to manage to do that. My body was fighting against me, determined to end my life without air. Not content until my chest had squeezed the very last millimetre of life-giving oxygen out of it. I hit dial, the last number belonging to the one person who knew what was really happening in my life. She picked up after only two rings.

'Helloooo,' she sang into the phone. At least she was in a good space. I couldn't answer. It felt like my head would explode. 'Ashray?' She was going to hang up thinking I had accidentally dialled her, but I couldn't speak. 'Unlock your door. I'm coming. Do you hear me, Ashray? Don't disconnect. Just breathe. I'm coming.' I pressed a key, hoping she would understand that this was an acknowledgement, a thank you from someone whose emotions had rendered him mute. To this day, I do not know how she got to me as quickly as she did, or why I had instinctively left my front door unlocked. It could have been a subconscious cry for company on the second-worst day of my life, but when she came running down the passage, I knew I would be okay.

'Ashray, look at me.' I fought my breathing, staring at the envelope in my hand. 'Ashray!' I looked up. 'Five things,' she continued. I nodded my head. 'Five things you see.' I began listing the things I could see, working through the process, By the time I reached the scent of the incense, I was telling her about how Maa and I would argue about which smelled better. She dabbed the sweat from my brow with the corner of her white sweater, sharing in my memories. Finally, when it was clear that the attack had passed, she said, 'Do you feel like some tea? Shall I make us some?'

'Yes,' I replied, 'but I want to sit here a little longer, if you don't mind?' She smiled at me, leaving me on the floor of the spare bedroom to go through my Maa's boxes. She returned with two mugs of tea. The sweet brew helping to calm what was left of my panic attack. I looked around the room at the three open boxes in front of me.

'Is this all there is, Jhanvi?' She looked at me, confused. 'Is this the sum total of our existence on earth? Three boxes?' Her confusion gave way to sadness. She took my hand and lead me to the bathroom that had never been used. Switching the lights on, the grey marble room came to life. She guided me to the mirror, but I looked down, not wanting to see the state I was in. Scared that seeing the effect that my panic attacks had on me would convince me that I was a mad man.

'Look, Ashray.' I shook my head. 'Please,' she whispered. I looked up; sad eyes stared back at me, but the face was the same, selfishly unchanged by the heartache and turmoil inside of me. '*You* are the sum total of her existence. She lived because of you, and she died because life is cruel. She isn't the boxes or the clothes or the memories you cling to, Ashray. She is you, and you are her, and you are so privileged. Do you know why?' I shook my head, not understanding what she was saying. 'You're privileged because you know without a shadow of a doubt that she loved you. Every breath she took, every moment of every day, she loved you because she chose to love you. You weren't born of her. She chose you, and she loved you. How beautiful, how magnificent is a love like that?' Tears flowed as I looked at myself, finally seeing what my Maa saw.

'I wish you could see how much you are loved, Ashray. By her, by Rishi, by me.' I held my breath at her accidental admittance to feeling for me what I felt for her.

'You love me?' I asked, when I probably shouldn't have, but I needed to draw from her strength; needed to know that I wasn't once again becoming attached to someone who would toss me aside.

'I wouldn't be here if I didn't.' She smiled sadly, not letting go of my shoulders, her eyes meeting mine in the mirror. 'But for now, we need to focus on ourselves don't you think? On learning to love what is inside us, the good and the bad, before we love anyone else.'

I nodded, knowing that what she said was true and accepting that if I just let her be, let myself be, that one day we may have our chance. She gave my shoulders a squeeze as a new wave of sadness washed over me.

'I don't know how to honour her,' I said quietly.

'That's easy,' she said and smiled as she referenced the phrase I used a few days earlier, 'you live your life in the way you promised her you would.'

'Where's your phone,' I asked her, suddenly noticing that she was not holding it.

'Someone wise once told me I needed to be present and detach myself from the noise it creates,' she said with a wink as we walked out of the bathroom. 'Hell of a place you have here.'

'Give you the tour?'

She laughed, linking her arm in mine. 'Go on.'

I led her to the living room, and then to the balcony where Maa was going to plant her chillies, telling her about all my plans for the place. Watching her eyes shine with excitement. The Mumbai skyline in the background. My future, in the foreground.

36

RISHI

Ashray was all the parts of me I fought to control.

From the moment I met him, nervous and unsure of himself on his first day at BusinessForward, I felt a connection to him that I knew would turn into a lifelong friendship. He lacked confidence, a trait I knew was rooted in his past, and confidence was not something I had ever lacked. Perhaps it was the fact that I grew up in a big family, where one had to be fought to be heard, that drove me to help him find his voice. Everything else I identified with. The deep need to be acknowledged and to know that I was seen and appreciated was perhaps the greatest affiliation I felt towards him. I had learned many years ago that my smile and carefree attitude were my greatest weapons in hiding my insecurities and, as I got older, I deployed them with frightening efficiency. The fact remained, though, that I too wanted to be needed, and the fear of rejection would always play a massive role in my ability to cope with what life threw my way.

With Ashray, I felt important, felt needed, and I enjoyed it in the beginning, perhaps serving my own selfish needs. As our friendship developed, I realised that I liked the guy. Truly liked him. I felt closer to him than I did to my own family; my siblings—now all scattered across the globe—usually got together once or twice a year in a raucous cacophony of who wanted to be heard first. With Ashray, I could be myself, could talk and actually be heard. He was a breath of fresh air, the male friend I never knew I needed.

I soon realised that Ashray was instrumental in me being able to heal myself from my past hurts, from my breakup, and from my parents being halfway across the world. He gave me a sense of belonging and a safe place I could call home. He was my person, the one human being who never judged me, yet somehow, I could never articulate that to him. I could never let him know how I felt. Expressing how I felt was never my strong point. For him, though, it seemed easy. He wore his heart on his sleeve, eagerly handing out his love in the same way I handed out cups of coffee in a bid to be liked or accepted.

When Sakshi came along, Ashray finally seemed completely content. A natural at his job, he flourished from day one, but with Sakshi by his side he seemed to finally have found his purpose. A drive to start the family he so desperately wanted. Not even once did I see their breakup coming. She seemed so sincere and so in love with him that I didn't think anything would drive them apart. Unfortunately, I had misread her.

I tried to help him pick up the pieces of his broken heart. I thought we had glued them back together quite well, until the night his Maa passed away. Like a freshly mended vase that is knocked too hard, his heart shattered once more. I could understand his pain; losing either one of my parents would, I imagine, devastate me to a point where I didn't know if I would recover. I watched my best friend fall apart, become a shell of the human being I once knew. I did everything I could. Everything I knew that would ease my pain, but Ashray spoke a different love language from me. Things didn't matter to him, I realised. What he wanted, needed from me were the words I found so difficult to express.

Latika, of course, berated me often for it, telling me that he needed me to be emotionally available, and I wanted to be. Really I did, but when his emotions overwhelmed him; when panic rose and anxiety forced the air from his lungs, I too would panic.

And then there was Jhanvi, a woman he met at his psychiatrist's office. I admit to being incredibly wary of her to begin with. Women like that didn't date men like Ashray and me. I recalled meeting her at the Goa Music Festival, and realised that our lives were intrinsically interwoven before we had ever fully known it. Jhanvi? Well, she was broken too. Broken in a different way, a way that Ashray found his purpose in, much in the same way I had found my purpose in him. I worried, though. Worried that he would invest all his time and effort in her only to be discarded when the next famous person flashed a smile her way.

Boy, was I wrong!

As their meetings became more frequent and I became more comfortable being around Ashray in his new and healing state, I saw something in him, something that was undeniable but that I would not pressure him about. His connection with Jhanvi gave way to something else. Something deeper. He looked at her in the same way that my father had spent his whole life looking at my mother. The way that I hoped I would one day look at Latika. And wouldn't you know it; she looked at him in the same way. But I also knew that, at this moment in life, they were on a different train, a different war waging within themselves, which I could never completely understand. Still, I couldn't help but be protective of him. I think I always will be, knowing what he has gone through. Experiencing the fragility of human life first-hand and understanding the consequences for those left behind.

One thing is certain though. One day, when I am as brave as my best friend, I will have the courage to say all of the things that have been left unspoken between us. For now, I only know how to show him with pats on the back and this new coffee-maker I got him for his apartment; but one day, not far from now, he will know how he healed me without even knowing it.

37

JHANVI

'I'm sorry what?' I thought I had heard him incorrectly.

'You're doing well, Jhanvi, I don't think you need to come to me anymore. But if you feel yourself slipping, or if for any reason you need help, you can make an appointment. You understand that your life doesn't revolve around your addiction anymore. You are using your affirmations, and your need to relapse is under control.' I nodded, agreeing with what he was saying, knowing it was the truth.

'So, that's it then?'

'You're using the techniques I have taught you very effectively, and you are more present and less concerned with what others think of you.' It was true; seeing Ashray falling apart, experiencing his pain first-hand, was the wakeup call I'd needed. Moving him through to the mirror and watching the profound impact acknowledging himself had on his well-being was enough to convince me that what the doctor had taught me worked.

Dr Shyam was right, it was time. My relationship with my mom and dad was great, they had even agreed to fly down for a weekend so that I could show them some of my favourite places in Mumbai. Kavya, under my instruction, had squeezed my schedule and, with a little bit of work, we were able to make sure that I no longer needed to work afterhours. No more club appearances, that wasn't the image I wanted to portray anymore. I wanted to be me, and those who wanted to follow were welcome to; those who didn't were free to walk their own path. I couldn't afford a relapse; didn't want to live through the hell I had lived through trying to wean myself off the highs that almost killed me. I understood that control was a farce, a mirage used by others to give the impression of perfection.

'Your friendship with Ashray has done you good. I'm happy that something positive has come from our sessions.' I stood up from the couch, taking in his room one last time before stretching out my hand to say goodbye. In the reception area, Ashray sat with his file of papers. I had learned a while back that they were portfolios for prospective clients. Lifting my hand to wave in his direction before giving the receptionist a hug, I saw the confusion on his face.

Walking out of the doctor's office, the Mumbai sky hung heavy with the start of the monsoon season. It felt like a lifetime ago that I had run in a torrential downpour, trying to escape my life, using the rain to hide my tears as they fell freely in response to Puneet's betrayal. So much had changed in the months that followed; I finally felt alive, accepted not only by those who loved me, but accepted by myself. I opened my phone, not to check my statistics, not to post a photo, but to phone my mom and let her know the good news.

As I disconnected the call, the first drops of rain began to fall. I sent Ashray a message, knowing that he would only get it when he was finished with Dr Shyam.

'Kavya and I are cooking tonight at your place, invite Rishi.'

The taxi was waiting for me as the heavens opened. A young woman made a mad dash towards the doors of the building I had just exited. Fear was written on her face, anxiety forcing her to claw her wet, clinging dress from her chest. Hopefully, Ashray would give her a comforting smile when he left so that she knew she wasn't alone in all of this. That she, too, could overcome it.

38

DR SHYAM

It isn't unusual for a relationship to develop between patients. People in need tend to lean on each other, the wounded often seeking out other wounded. Even in the animal kingdom, the sick finds the sick, the dying somehow instinctively seeking out the resting place of those who have passed before them. In people who have come to me or any other professional, this is not necessarily a good thing, and so, when Jhanvi and Ashray's friendship initially blossomed, I tentatively warned them against it. They proved me wrong though. Ashray, ever wise, told me that two slightly damaged planks laid with their faults in opposing directions would still hold more weight than one thin plank. In this instance, he was right; they complemented each other in a way I could never have expected and, I am sure, have had many a laugh and complaint session about me. Regardless, considering the level of anxiety both Jhanvi and Ashray displayed when first walking into my office, I have been impressed with the progress they have made.

Jhanvi, always resistant as she is, was a challenge. Her need for perfection so deep-seated in her created identity that it was tough to get her to separate herself from her perceived reality. I ultimately found that challenging her ideals pushed her to be present, and to accept that not everything in life can be controlled to the extent that she expected it to be. Still, I believe she will always have to fight her need to be perfect, to separate herself from the two-dimensional world she is immersed in. I am not a fan of social media, but I cannot deny that it has its place and can be used for good. With hard work and the tools I have given her, she could have the right kind of impact on others. Hopefully, there will come a day when she understands that mental health issues do not make you weak, they are not a stigma; they are prevalent, and should be spoken about. There should be loud proclamations from rooftops or, in Jhanvi's case, through her influence, telling others that it is okay to be less than perfect. That reaching out and seeking help is not weakness. It is strength.

And Ashray? He is proof that life is sometimes nothing more than a roll of the dice. A game played by fate in which some win and some lose, but no one loses forever; even the unluckiest player will throw a winning number once in a while. Ashray needed to learn that losing didn't mean that he was lost, and that winning was not defined by how much, or how little others loved him. It was important for Ashray to see that his wisdom and the gentleness inside him were also by-products of his tough childhood. I don't think a child ever quite gets over the sense of abandonment that comes with being left in an orphanage. For those who are able to make peace with the circumstances, it may be easier. But for him, and for all the others, the sense of abandonment forms their core and it will never be replaced. The best they can do is to work through that, to find a way to know without a shadow of a doubt that they do not have control over the actions of others. That life is sometimes cruel and that the only thing we can control is how we react; how we pick ourselves up and take the steps towards healing. His panic attacks were a direct manifestation of his belief that he couldn't possibly make the decisions required to live his life well without the advice and approval of others. How ironic, though, that he would later come to understand that it was his advice and his approval that helped others.

But I digress. Jhanvi and Ashray, combined, two slightly damaged planks laid in opposite directions, bore the weight of their illness. They leaned on each other when the pressure was too much for one of them to handle, and they made it through by finding the one thing that every human being needs.

Love.

39

ASHRAY

The sound of laughter filled my apartment. In the living room, Rishi and Kavya were talking animatedly. In the kitchen, Jhanvi stirred a pot of stew that she admitted was already mostly premade and bought from the supermarket near her apartment.

'So, that's us healed then?' she asked, looking up from the stove.

'Well,' I replied, unsure if there would ever be a time when we would be completely healed.

'Oh! Before I forget—' she said and, reaching into her bag on the counter, she pulled out a gift bag and handed it to me. 'I saw these and thought they would look amazing on your shelves in the kitchen.' I opened the bag. Inside were the colourful pots Maa and I had seen at the market. The ones I'd made a mental note to buy for her once we had moved into our new apartment. 'Ashray?' I stood open-mouthed as she asked me, 'Did I do something wrong?'

'No,' I said with a smile, pulling her into a hug, 'they're absolutely perfect.' I unpacked them and asked her to place them on the shelves. She was right. They did look beautiful, offset by the white background.

'So, are we going to eat this food that Jhanvi slaved over the supermarket counter to buy?' Rishi called out.

Jhanvi threw a dishcloth at him, causing him to double over, faking a mortal wound. Kavya and I laughed at the two of them playfully bantering with each other. Jhanvi was right. I was the sum total of my Maa's existence, and this moment would have made her proud, not just of me but of my friends too. That

I was living my life, our dreams, with people who loved me and wanted to be in my life. The night of my last panic attack, Jhanvi had helped me put a picture of Maa in a frame, and it now stood on the floating shelf near the flat-screen television. I stood in front of her smiling face, taking a moment to look into her eyes, hearing the laughter filtering from my balcony. Jhanvi's familiar hand touched my back in the way that had become a comfortable gesture of love and affection between us.

'You okay?' I turned and smiled at her.

'I'm perfect,' I said, knowing that, without a shadow of a doubt, I was.

EPILOGUE

'Life & People', a support group, was put together not only in memory of Ashray's Maa, but in honour of all those brave souls struggling to make it through the challenges in their lives. It came to us one night when I was feeling low. I turned to Ashray, questioning him about the purpose of my life. He admitted that he often felt the same way. Life was good, we had nothing to complain about, but somehow, leaving Dr Shyam's office, watching the young woman dashing for the door, bewildered and alone, left a lasting impression. Our story wasn't complete; our personal pain had a meaning, a purpose outside of teaching us to take better care of ourselves. What if everyone had a Kavya, a Rishi, a Jhanvi or an Ashray? What if there was one person who could hold your hand to the doctor's office door, or who would pull you out of bed with the promise that tomorrow would be better? If you knew that someone could help you through your treatment, without judgement, with understanding and love, someone who could hear what your heart was saying and embrace it through all the noise?

I always wondered what my purpose was, outside of the path I had chosen, outside of the noise and the disposable life I had created. And now, in the community centre hall, as I watched Ashray speaking to a group of people, smiling kindly, reassuring them, I knew what it was. My pain and my healing had a purpose and that was the best I could have hoped for as I continued my journey to becoming whole again. He always spoke of his Maa's ability to give advice, but he was really good at it too. As for me, I was there more to comfort those who broke down, bringing them back from the brink. The physical touch I so desperately craved, I wanted to give to others. I wanted to give them strength, and to let them know that they were loved. Human contact, I had learned, was how I expressed my love, and once I was able to receive love, I was able to give it freely.

It was a year-and-a-half since my breakdown. A year-and-a-half of recovery. The journey continued, together with my parents' blessings, and the support of Kavya and Ashray. Finally, I understood that by surrounding myself with good people, people who lifted me instead of judging me, I could shine through the darkness that society emitted so readily.

'Excuse me.' A young girl stood before me, tugging on her sleeves, her hair hanging in her face. I brushed it away from her eyes, encouraging her to look at me. 'I just wanted to thank you for this group. I have no one, and without you all, I don't know how I could possibly get through this.' I put my hand on her arm, reassuring her that we were there for her. No matter what, we would be her lifeline. 'What about you? After your boyfriend cheated on you and after you have healed, do you think you could love again?' I smiled at her, knowing that my answer could have a profound impact on this young woman's life. An impact that was more than a two-dimensional image on a screen.

'It will come, at the right time, with the right person, it will come, but for now,' I looked her in the eyes, 'for now, I live each day for what it is, knowing that I am present enough to accept love when it finds me.' Her eyes filled with tears, a deep hurt inside of her bubbling to the surface.

'Some days, I don't know if I can get through this. If I am even worthy of love. I want to believe that I am but ...' She didn't finish her sentence. Didn't need to. I understood the yearning for acceptance, the feeling of not being enough.

'You have to love yourself first,' I said, patting her arm, encouraging her to open up to me.

'I try,' she said, 'I do try to tell myself I am worthy, but it's difficult. You know.' I pulled her into me, embracing her tightly.

Walking out of the community centre together, Ashray lifted his eyebrows at me.

'You're looking happy with yourself.' Lately, his smile came much more easily.

'It was a good day,' I said.

'Yes. A good day. Is that young woman okay?'

'She will be, when,' I looked at him, hoping he would understand, 'when she is ready to love herself.'

'Just like you, then?'

'Yes, just like me.' I smiled.

'And do you love yourself, Jhanvi?' It didn't take much thought this time, I didn't need to find the reasons why I was worthy of love.

'Yes.'

'I would call that a breakthrough,' he said, as he smiled and reached out, pulling my hand into his.

We walked the path to the main road together in silence, our fingers intertwined. Willing to accept love, willing to give love, willing to truly understand that we are never alone if we allow ourselves to just love.

TO MY READERS

To the ones who, like Jhanvi, have lost themselves trying to be someone else—please know that you too will find your way back. After the storm and chaos, peace and happiness will return.

To the ones who, like Ashray, have gone through tragic and painful heartbreaks and loss—I want you to still believe that the universe has planned a beautiful end for you. Please don't give up yet.

To the ones who, like Rishi and Kavya, are kind and compassionate and are the best examples of friendship—thank you for being such beautiful souls. The world needs more people like you.

To my readers, who have patiently waited for this book—you have no idea how thankful I am to you. You are the reason I can continue doing what I love.

Thank you for sharing your lives with me, writing me encouraging emails and critical feedback, recommending my books to others and interacting with me on social media.

If you loved this book and have a minute to spare, I would really appreciate a short review on the page or site where you bought the book. Your help in spreading the word is greatly appreciated.

You're all amazing!

With profound gratitude,
Savi

ACKNOWLEDGEMENTS

First and above all, I praise the Universe for guiding me towards the purpose of my life.

A big thanks to my family and friends for their love, support and trust in me.

Special mention to Deepthi Talwar, my sweet editor, for saving me the embarrassment of making terrible mistakes. Thank you, Neha Khanna, for not just being an amazing author relationship manager, but a beautiful soul sister.

I am grateful to the entire team at HarperCollins India, for their untiring efforts in helping my stories reach you.

Thank you, Ashish Bagrecha, my partner in stories and now my partner in life. I am so blessed to have you.

ABOUT THE AUTHOR

On a mission to inspire millions of people through her writings, Savi Sharma Bagrecha left her CA studies to become a writer. She is the author of *Everyone Has a Story – 1*, its sequel *Everyone Has a Story – 2*, and *This Is Not Your Story*. With combined sales of over 6 lakh copies, she is currently India's highest-selling female author.

Inspired from real-life experiences, her books revolve around the themes of dreams, hope, courage, friendship, love and the Universe, with the aim of filling young readers with positivity and happiness.

She is also a motivational speaker and has delivered inspiring talks on different topics at the IIMs, IITs, popular literature festivals and other esteemed organisations.

Married to Ashish Bagrecha, another best-selling author, she currently resides in Surat.

Savi dreams of a world full of kindness, compassion, empathy and love.

You can connect with her on www.savisharma.com or follow @storytellersavi on Facebook, Twitter and Instagram.

A MUST READ

If you are someone struggling with depression, negativity, anxiety, heartbreak or loss, I'd strongly recommend you read *Dear Stranger, I Know How You Feel*, a self-help book written by my mentor, husband and best-selling author Ashish Bagrecha.

This book is filled with so much hope and positivity, and provides a very intimate insight into the process of recovery and healing.

You can get this book on Amazon, Flipkart and bookstores near you.

30 Years *of*

 HarperCollins *Publishers* India

At HarperCollins, we believe in telling the best stories and finding the widest possible readership for our books in every format possible. We started publishing 30 years ago; a great deal has changed since then, but what has remained constant is the passion with which our authors write their books, the love with which readers receive them, and the sheer joy and excitement that we as publishers feel in being a part of the publishing process.

Over the years, we've had the pleasure of publishing some of the finest writing from the subcontinent and around the world, and some of the biggest bestsellers in India's publishing history. Our books and authors have won a phenomenal range of awards, and we ourselves have been named Publisher of the Year the greatest number of times. But nothing has meant more to us than the fact that millions of people have read the books we published, and somewhere, a book of ours might have made a difference.

As we step into our fourth decade, we go back to that one word – a word which has been a driving force for us all these years.

Read.

Harper
Collins

HARPER
PERENNIAL

HARPER
BUSINESS

HARPER
BLACK

हार्पर
हिन्दी

HarperCollins
Children's Books

HARPER
DESIGN

HARPER
VANTAGE

Harper
Sport